Illustrated Tales from
Indian Mythology

Wonder House

Wonder House

(An imprint of Prakash Books)

contact@wonderhousebook.com

ISBN : 978-93-54403-97-2

This book belongs to

. . . .

Contents

Arjuna Takes Aim at Bird

Dronacharya was the tutor of the princes of Hastinapur. One day, he asked his students to aim their arrows at a wooden bird hung on a tree.

Before they could proceed, Dronacharya asked Duryodhana, "What do you see?"

Duryodhana replied, "I can see the bird, the tree, the flowers and the grass."

Dronacharya told him to step aside. Similarly, he asked his other students and got identical responses. "What do you see?" he asked Arjuna in the end.

At once, Arjuna replied, "I see the bird's eye!"

Surprised, Dronacharya asked again, "Don't you see the tree, the grass, the sun or me?"

"No, I only see the bird's eye," said Arjuna.

Dronacharya smiled and asked Arjuna to release the arrow. Arjuna's aim hit its target. Dronacharya praised Arjuna and said, "Always remember, focus is the key to excellence!"

Arjuna Saves Dronacharya

Once, Dronacharya heard the twang of a bowstring around midnight. Curious, he stepped out of his hut and went in the direction of the sound. To his surprise, he found Arjuna practicing archery. He was pleased with his dedication.

A few days later, Dronacharya was bathing in the river near his hermitage, when a crocodile attacked him. He could have rescued himself easily but instead, he decided to test the skills of his students. All the princes except Arjuna, panicked and were clueless how to rescue their teacher. However, Arjuna swiftly picked up his bow and calmly shot five arrows to subdue the crocodile and freed his teacher.

Dronacharya stepped out of the river and approached Arjuna. He said, "I am pleased with your reflexes and skills. As a reward, I will give you the divine weapon Brahmashira."

Draupadi's Swayamvar

King Draupada, mighty ruler of Panchala, invited several kings and princes to attend his daughter Draupadi's Swayamvar. King Draupada welcomed everyone and announced, "A pole has been affixed in the middle of a water bowl. On top of that pole, on a rotating disc is a wooden fish. The one, who can pierce the eye of the fish by looking at its reflection in the water bowl, will be deemed worthy of marrying Draupadi."

One by one, the invited kings tried their luck, but no one was successful.

Finally, Arjuna who was disguised as a Brahmin stepped forward. He picked up the bow and arrow placed near the water bowl and took his aim. To everybody's surprise, Arjuna's arrow pierced the fish's eye. Princess Draupadi was married to Arjuna. It was later revealed to King Draupada that the Brahmin was Arjuna in disguise. The reluctant father was elated hearing this.

Khandav Van

Arjuna and Krishna were staying in Indraprastha, the Pandava capital, when a sage approached them and sought their help.

Arjuna replied, "O sage, tell us how we can help you?"

Assured thus, the sage revealed his true identity and said, "I am Agni, the fire god. I am starving and I seek your help in burning Khandav forest to satiate my hunger. Khandav forest, home to many beasts, is destined to die with my flames. However the snake god Takshaka, Lord Indra's dear friend, lives in that forest. So, every time I try to burn down the forest, Lord Indra sends a deluge."

Arjuna said, 'O Agni, I have knowledge of the celestial weapons but I lack a powerful bow to fight Lord Indra."

So, the fire god gave a bow named Gandiva to Arjuna. Armed thus, Arjuna and Krishna went to the forest. Once there, Agni began to ravage the forest while Arjuna and Krishna kept a lookout for Lord Indra.

Arjuna used his Gandiva bow to make a layer of arrows on top of the forest in such fashion that not even a single drop of water could reach the forest. A fierce battle took place where Krishna and Arjuna fought Indra valiantly. At last, a divine voice stopped the battle. It said, "Indra stop! Your friend Takshaka and his family are safe and have escaped the forest. Let Agni devour it."

The battle stopped and Agni satiated his hunger.

A asura named Mayasura also resided in the Khandav forest. When Takshaka fled from the forest, Mayasura approached Arjuna to spare his life. Arjuna did likewise.

As a sign of gratitude, Mayasura constructed a mystical palace of illusions for the Pandavas.

Urvashi's Curse

When the Pandavas were exiled after losing the game of dice, Lord Indra summoned Arjuna to his abode. During his stay, Indra gifted Arjuna several celestial weapons and taught him powerful mantras to invoke them.

During his stay in Indra's abode, Arjuna also learnt the art of music and dancing from a Gandharva named Chitrasena. One day, when Arjuna went to his room after his practice, he found Urvashi, a celestial nymph, waiting for him.

Seeing him, she said, "Dear Arjuna, I have fallen in love with you. I have never met someone so strong and attractive. Please accept me as your lover!"

Arjuna was shocked and replied, "I can't accept your proposal. Please forgive me. You are as sacred to me as my mother."

Urvashi unable to take Arjuna's rejection, cursed him in fury, "I am no one's mother! For your rude treatment, I curse you to live your life as a eunuch."

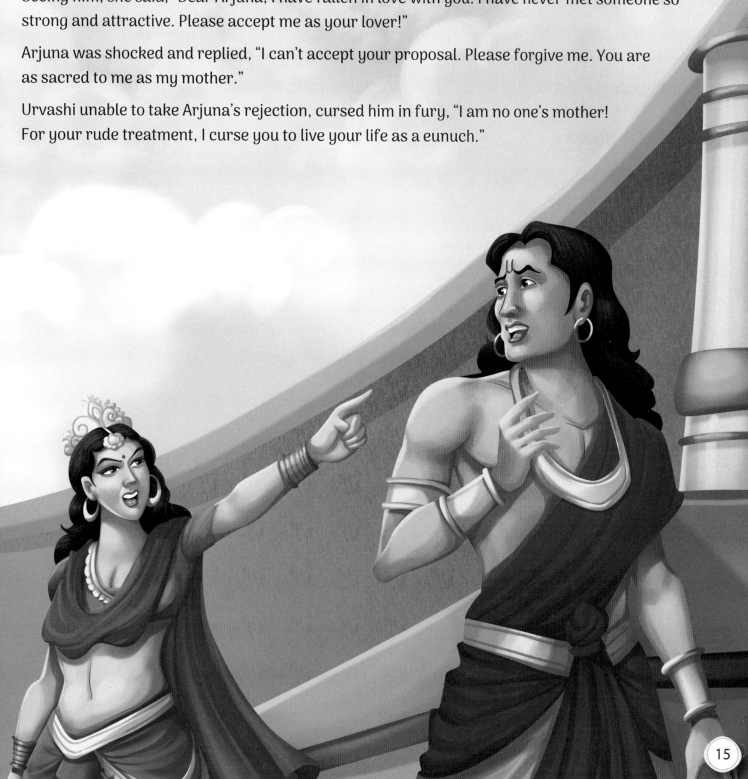

Arjuna was devastated hearing Urvashi's curse. Learning of the incident, Indra requested Urvashi, saying, "Urvashi, curtail your curse and make it last for only one year. Your curse will thus help Arjuna stay disguised during their year of incognito."

Urvashi agreed and modified her curse. Soon, Arjuna returned to earth.

During the thirteenth year of their exile, Pandavas came to the Matsya kingdom. In this year they had to keep themselves hidden. So, they took up odd jobs for the royal family. Draupadi became the queen's attendant while Bhima began working in the royal kitchen. Yudhisthira became a counselor to King Virat.

Arjuna became a eunuch named Brihannala and was the dance teacher of Princess Uttara.

One day, the queen's brother Kichaka tried to harass Draupadi. When Bhima learnt of the incident, he killed Kichaka. When Duryodhana learnt about Kichaka's death, he suspected that the Pandavas were in Matsya kingdom.

Arjuna Fights as Brihannala

Pandavas thirteenth year of exile was almost over. On Duryodhana's request, Matsya kingdom was attacked by one of its neighboring kingdoms. King Virat led an army to the battlefield. All the Pandavas except Arjuna joined him. In his absence, his son, Prince Uttar, took care of the kingdom.

One day, Prince Uttar learnt that Hastinapur's army was about to attack his kingdom. So, the prince wasted no time and prepared for war. Arjuna, who by now had gained the trust of the royal family, volunteered to be his charioteer.

When Prince Uttar reached the battlefield, he became numb seeing the massive Kaurava army and the elite warriors in their ranks.

He said, "I cannot fight these mighty warriors alone. Brihannala, let's go back and save our lives while we still can!"

Brihannala refused and said, "The onus of saving your kingdom lies on your shoulders. If you run away from this battle, you will be called a coward."

Brihannala then revealed her true identity as Arjuna and said, "Come with me, Prince Uttar. Let me fetch my Gandiva and fight this battle for you."

Arjuna took Uttar to a nearby tree and dug out the mighty weapons of the Pandavas hidden there. Uttar became Arjuna's charioteer while Arjuna announced his arrival with the twang of his bow. The Kaurava army immediately realized that Pandavas' exile was over and that Arjuna was before them.

Arjuna won the battle single-handedly for Matsya kingdom. Also, filled with gratitude, King Virat married his daughter to Arjuna's son, Abhimanyu.

Arjuna and Hanuman

During exile, Arjuna visited Rameshwar. He was observing the remains of Rama Setu when an old monkey startled him by asking, "Why are you staring at the bridge?"

Arjuna replied, "Lord Rama was a legendary archer. I was wondering why didn't he build a bridge with his arrows."

The monkey smiled and said, "A bridge of arrows! Such a bridge could never have withstood the weight of the mighty Vanara army. Such a bridge can't even hold my weight."

Arjuna felt challenged and created a bridge with arrows. He then challenged the monkey to prove him wrong. The bridge crumbled the moment the monkey stepped on it. Arjuna tried again after praying to Krishna and the bridge remained intact when the monkey stepped on it.

Suddenly, the monkey transformed into Lord Hanuman and said, "You have learned your lesson, Arjuna. You should be confident but not arrogant."

Arjuna humbled, bowed to Lord Hanuman.

Arjuna Defeats Bhishma

During the battle of Kurukshetra, Bhishma was the commander of the Kaurava army. Bhishma wreaked havoc on the Pandava's army on the ninth day of the battle. Lord Krishna was furious at Arjuna's inability to defeat Bhishma.

He chided Arjuna, "You are reluctant to kill Bhishma while he is destroying our army. If you cannot do it, I will do it myself!"

Saying this, Krishna picked up a chariot wheel to attack Bhishma. Arjuna begged Krishna, "Lord, you took a vow to refrain from taking up arms in this battle. Please don't break your vow. I will find a way to stop Bhishma."

Finally Krishna relented. At the end of the day's battle, Krishna suggested a plan to the Pandavas, saying, "Bhishma has a boon to choose the time of his death. We must approach Bhishma and ask him to share the secret of defeating him."

That night Krishna and the Pandavas went to Bhishma's tent. They requested him to reveal the means of killing him. Bhishma replied, "You have a eunuch warrior named Shikhandi who was a woman in previous birth. I will not shoot an arrow in her direction."

On the tenth day of the war, Shikhandi rode on Arjuna's chariot and they approached Bhishma. Bhishma put down his weapons. Using this opportunity, Arjuna pierced Bhishma's body with a volley of arrows. Bhishma fell on the ground with arrows sticking out of his back. He remained likewise till the end of the war. The warring armies stopped fighting when he fell. Arjuna apologised to Bhishma for defeating him in an unfair fight but Bhishma said, "Don't regret Arjuna. This is my fate and I accept it." After a while, he said, "I am thirsty."

Arjuna shot an arrow towards the ground. A jet of water from River Ganga shot up from the ground and quenched Bhishma's thirst.

Arjuna Slays Jaydratha

Lord Shiva had granted Jaydratha, the Sindhu king, a boon that he could defeat all Pandavas except Arjuna for one day. Due to this, Jaydratha managed to stop the Pandavas from entering the Chakravyuh as Abhimanyu, Arjuna's son fought the Kauravas alone.

Arjuna was furious on learning about Abhimanyu's death. He took a terrible oath, "I will kill Jaydratha by sunset tomorrow or else I will kill myself."

The next day, Arjuna was unable to reach Jaydratha for he was craftly protected by the Kauravas. Krishna, then, played a trick. He hid the sun behind the clouds, giving everyone the impression that the sun had set. Thinking himself to be safe, Jaydratha came out of his security cordon. Krishna smiled and cleared the sky once again. The sun came out. At once, Arjuna released an arrow and beheaded Jaydratha, fulfilling his vow.

Arjuna Kills Karna

On the seventeenth day of the war, Arjuna came face to face with Karna. Soon, they engaged in a fierce battle.

A snake named Ashwasena, who sought revenge against Arjuna for killing his mother, crawled into Karna's quiver and turned itself into an arrow. Karna took out that arrow and shot it at Arjuna.

Krishna realized that the arrow was Ashwasena and could kill Arjuna. He pressed down the chariot with his foot causing it to sink into the ground. The arrow missed its mark and struck Arjuna's crown instead, knocking it off his head.

The crown turned to dust. The battle between the two warriors commenced again.

Every time Arjuna struck Karna's chariot with his arrows, it would go back several meters. However, Karna's arrows managed to send Arjuna's chariot back by few feet. Arjuna was surprised when Krishna praised Karna's valor. Krishna explained, "Arjuna, Your chariot is protected by Hanuman and me and yet Karna manages to move it. In our absence, Karna would have destroyed your chariot."

In time, Karna tried to summon Brahmastra, his ultimate weapon. But he was unable to remember the mantra to invoke it due to a curse. Further, the wheel of Karna's chariot got stuck in the mud due to Earth goddess' curse. Karna himself got down to push out the wheel. Krishna advised Arjuna to use that opportunity to kill Karna. Initially, Arjuna refused to strike an unarmed warrior but on Krishna's behest Arjuna killed mighty Karna.

Matsya Avatar

Hayagriva was a horse-faced demon. He was the son of Sage Kashyapa and his wife, Danu. Unlike his virtuous father, Hayagriva made several attempts to empower the danavs. During one such attempt, he stole the four sacred Vedas from Brahmaloka and hid them deep under the ocean. However, Lord Vishnu had seen Hayagriva steal the Vedas and decided to get them back.

He decided on a plan and sought pious Sage Satyavrata also known as Manu. He thought, "He is the ideal person to carry out my plan."

One morning, as Satyavrata went to Krithamala river to offer his morning prayers, when a tiny fish swam into his hands and pleaded with him to save its life.

Manu was merciful. He put the fish into a jar, which it soon outgrew. He then moved it to a tank, a river and finally put it in the ocean.
To his surprise, the fish continued to grow.

"Who are you?" asked Sage Satyavrata. The fish replied, "I am Vishnu. A deluge will occur after seven days and it will destroy all life. Collect the best of seeds and the best pair of animals. Summon the seven great sages and build a large ship." The fish was Lord Vishnu's Matsya avatar.

On the seventh day, the great floods started swallowing the earth. Sage Satyavrata, the seven great sages along with the animals and grains were already on the ship. Soon, the great fish appeared and brought with it the snake, Vasuki.

The fish tied the ship to itself using Vasuki as a rope. Lord Vishnu, in his avatar, also imparted the knowledge of the Vedas to the seven sages. Before the deluge had started, Lord Vishnu in his Matsya avatar had dived deep, killed Hayagriva and gave the Vedas to Lord Brahma. After the deluge subsided, the ship anchored and life began again.

Kurma Avatar

Once, the short-tempered Sage Durvasa saw Indra, riding his elephant. Durvasa offered a garland of flowers to Indra. Now, Indra was too proud of his wealth and power. He placed the garland on the trunk of his elephant. The fragrance of the flowers intoxicated the elephant and he trampled the garland under its feet.

Angry Durvasa cursed Indra, "I curse you to lose your power and wealth."

Indra was repentant but Sage Durvasa was gone. Shortly afterward, the asuras attacked Indra's kingdom and won an easy victory over the weakened devas.

The exiled devas approached Lord Vishnu for help. Lord Vishnu replied, "Make a truce with the asuras. Ask for their help to churn the ocean of milk to obtain amrit. We will pretend to share it with them."

Indra approached the king of the asuras and said, "King Bali, I have a proposition for you. If you agree to churn the ocean of milk to procure the nectar of immortality, we will share it with you."

Bali agreed to help the devas but secretly he planned to take it for the asuras. With great effort the devas and the asuras carried Mount Mandara to the ocean of milk to use it as a churning device. Serpent Vasuki became the rope to churn the mountain.

Lord Vishnu, then transformed into a gigantic tortoise and supported the mountain on his back, to prevent it from sinking.

Halahal

Proud asuras held the head portion of Vasuki. At last the churning began. In time, the asuras were weakened by the poisonous fumes and fire emerging from Vasuki's head.

Soon, the churning produced a deadly poison called Halahal that threatened to destroy the entire universe. It was then that Lord Shiva came and drank it. Goddess Parvati stopped the poison from going below his neck. As a result, the poison turned Lord Shiva's neck blue, earning him the name 'Nilakanta'.

All who were gathered thanked Lord Shiva for protecting the universe.

Churning of the Ocean

The devas and the asuras resumed the churning of the milky waters. Several precious objects and entities emerged from the ocean. These included the Parijata tree, the moon, the four-tusked white elephant Airavata, magical cow Kaamdhenu, Varuni the goddess of wine, the wish-fulfilling tree Kalpavriksha, divine horse Uccaihshravas, celestial dancers or apsaras, the conch Panchajanya, the divine bow Saranga and precious jewels like Kaustubha. All these entities were divided between devas, asuras, Lord Shiva and Lord Vishnu.

Goddess Lakshmi also emerged from the ocean. She chose Lord Vishnu to be her husband and married him. At last Dhanvantri, the divine physician, emerged from the ocean. He carried a golden pot filled with nectar. The asuras shoved aside the devas and took hold of the nectar.

Mohini

Lord Vishnu then assumed the form of an exquisitely beautiful woman, Mohini. Mohini approached the asuras, who were enamored by her beauty. They gave her the pot and asked her to divide it among them.

Mohini seated the asuras and the devas in two different rows. Mohini created an illusion for the asuras and began serving the nectar to the devas.

Now, a clever asura, Swarbhanu, quietly disguised himself as a deva and succeeded in drinking a few drops of nectar. The imposter was spotted and Lord Vishnu beheaded him using his discus. His head became Rahu and his body became Ketu.

After drinking the nectar, the devas regained their strength and defeated the asuras, forcing them to go into exile.

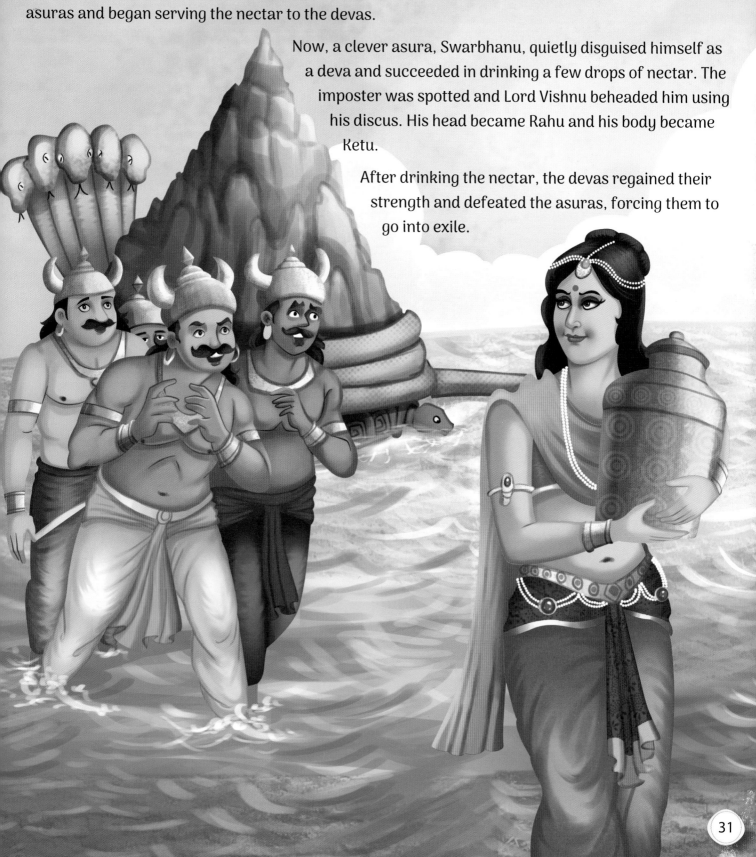

Varaha Avatar

During the Satya Yuga, Sage Kashyap and his wife Diti had two sons—Hiranyaksha and Hiranyakshipu. Hiranyaksha was a great devotee of Lord Brahma. Due to the latter's boon, he could not be killed by devas, humans and several beasts. Due to his newfound strength, Hiranyaksha defeated the devas. As the devas got strength from the offering made by humans on earth, he pushed Bhoomi Devi or Mother Earth to Pataal Lok, deep underneath the ocean.

As Brahma meditated on Lord Vishnu to protect Bhoomi Devi, a varaha or a tiny boar fell from his nostrils and started growing. The giant boar dived into the ocean and found Bhoomi Devi.

The boar was none other than Lord Vishnu. He lifted Bhoomi Devi and began swimming towards the surface. When Hiranyaksha found about Lord Vishnu's attempt to rescue Bhoomi Devi, he rushed towards the boar. He challenged the boar to fight him, but the boar ignored his threats and continued moving towards the surface.

The Varaha avatar brought Bhoomi Devi out of the water and gently placed her in her axis. He then turned to face Hiranyaksha and an intense duel began. Suddenly Lord Brahma warned Vishnu, "Kill Hiranyaksha before sunset or his powers will magnify manifold at night."

The boar, without waiting, unleashed several blows on Hiranyaksha's chest and killed him instantly.

Narsimha Avatar

Hiranyakashya's elder brother, Hiranyakshipu swore to avenge the death of his brother. He pleased Lord Brahma and sought a boon saying, "Grant me that I cannot be killed by man, beast, asuras or devas. That I cannot die during the day or at night. I can't die by the use of steel or stone or wood. I can't die indoors or outdoors, or on earth or sky."

After he got the boon Hiranyakshipu became a tyrant across all the lands. He banned the worship of Lord Vishnu and all other gods.

Unlike Hiranyakshipu, his son Prahlad, was a great devotee of Lord Vishnu. When Prahlad did not heed to his words, Hiranyakshipu asked his sister Holika to kill Prahlad. Holika had a gift that she would not burn in fire. She sat on a pyre with Prahlad in her lap. But Lord Vishnu protected Prahlad and instead Holika died.

Furious, Hiranyakshipu asked Prahlad to call Lord Vishnu. Prahlad told him that the Lord was everywhere. He is even in this pillar.

Hiranyakshipu retorted, "Then ask him to appear from this pillar."

Suddenly there was a thunderous boom and a ferocious being who was half man and half lion emerged from the pillar. The creature screamed, "I am Narasimha!"

Narsimha attacked Hiranyakshipu and dragged him to the threshold of the palace . He put him on his lap, where he was neither on earth or in sky. When Narsimha had appeared, it was twilight and nor was Hiranyakshipu inside or outside his house. Narsimha then pierced his nails into Hiranyakshipu's body and killed him without using any weapons. Narsimha had fulfilled all the conditions to bring an end to Hiranyakshipu.

Vamana Avatar

One day, Bali, Prahlada's grandson, went to meet Rishi Sukracharya, the guru of asuras. He asked, "How can I defeat the devas?"

Sukracharya advised him to perform the Vishwajeet yagya. After Bali performed the yagya, he became powerful and defeated the devas.

Meanwhile, Indra's mother Aditi, prayed to Lord Vishnu to help the devas. Lord Vishnu appeared and assured her that he would take birth as her son and cause Bali's downfall. In time, Aditi gave birth to a boy and named him Vamana because he was a dwarf. One day Vamana posed as a Brahmin and approached Bali as he performed a yagna.

Bali welcomed Vamana respectfully and asked, "What can I give you, young Brahmin?"

Vamana smiled and said, "I merely need the land that I can cover with my three strides."

Sukracharya, who had seen through Vamana's disguise, warned Bali, "He is not an ordinary Brahmin. He is Lord Vishnu. Retract your promise."

But Bali was firm on keeping his promise. An angry Sukracharya went away.

To Bali's surprise, the boy started to grow in size the next minute and became massive. In his first step, he claimed the Earth. In the second, he claimed Amravati.

Then, turning to Bali, Vamana said, "Bali, where should I keep my third step?"

Bali was humbled and he said, "You can keep your third step on my head."

On hearing Bali's words, Lord Vishnu appeared in his true form. He blessed Bali, "You kept your promise under such adversity. From now on, you will rule Pataal Loka." And Indra regained his lost kingdom.

Parshuram Rescues Kamdhenu

Lord Vishnu took birth as Parshuram, the youngest son of Sage Jamadagni. Despite being the son of a sage, Parshuram learnt warfare and became a fierce warrior.

One day evil King Arjuna along with his army visited the ashram of Sage Jamadagni. Sage Jamadagni welcomed everyone and served them milk. King Arjuna was fascinated by the cow, Kamdhenu which had provided milk for everyone instantly. He took away the cow and her calf forcefully.

When Parshuram learnt of the incident, he was furious and swore, "I will end the reign of Arjuna and all evil kings on earth!"

Parshuram killed King Arjuna and brought Kamdhenu and her calf back to the ashram.

Parshuram Curses Karna

After, Dronacharya, the teacher of Hastinapur princes refused to teach him archery, Karna approached Parshuram. Since Parshuram taught archery only to Brahmins, Karna lied and told Parshuram that he was a Brahmin.

Over the next few years, Parshuram trained Karna in warfare and taught him the mantras to call on celestial weapons. One day, Parshuram was sleeping under a tree while his head rested on Karna's lap. Suddenly an insect bit Karna's thigh and blood started to flow. Karna endured the pain as he did not intend to disturb his teacher.

When Parshuram woke up, he saw the blood and said, "Only a Kshatriya can endure such pain. I curse you that you shall forget all my teachings in the most crucial battle of your life."

Karna was repentant and apologized. He then blessed Karna, "You shall gain eternal glory for your skills and character."

Annapurna

One day, Shiva and Goddess Parvati played a game of dice and got into an argument. Suddenly, Lord Vishnu appeared and said, "The dice was moving according to my wish, and both of you were just under an illusion that you were in charge of the game."

Shiva replied, "Everything around us is an illusion. All worldly things, even the food we eat."

Hearing this, Goddess Parvati became furious. In order to prove that food was not maya, she disappeared. With her disappearance the fields became barren and infertile, causing acute droughts and a massive scarcity of food. Upon hearing the endless prayers of gods, asuras, and humans, Goddess Parvati appeared in Kashi and began distributing food. One day, Shiva appeared before Parvati holding a begging bowl.

He said, "I am nothing without you, and I have realized my mistake. Food is highly vital for the body as well as for the inner soul."

Since then, Parvati is also worshipped as Annapurna Devi—The Goddess of food.

Shiva Pacifies Goddess Kali

Goddess Kali saved the world by taking the life out of evil Raktabeej and lifted him towards the sky to drink his blood. Heavily drunk on the blood of triumph, the effects of Raktabeej's blood caused her to dance wildly. Unable to restrain herself, she made the world stutter again. The skies grew dark with her shrill laughter, and nothing seemed to stop her.

Afraid that the world would collapse, the gods prayed to Shiva, "O Lord! We beg you, please do something, or everything will be ruined."

Shiva tried to intervene and called out to her repeatedly, but she continued her thrashing, laughing and danced away. In an attempt to stop her, Shiva threw himself in her way. Still dancing, she stepped on her husband. It took Kali a few moments to realize who she had stepped on. Looking at Shiva, she immediately stopped her dance of devastation and became calm.

Saraswati and Gandharvas

There was a potion that the gods treasured known as Somras; the elixir of life. It was kept in a pitcher. A race of demigods, the Gandharvas, were entrusted with keeping it safe. Once, a Gandharva, Vishvavasu, became very curious about it.

Unable to control his desire, he stole the pitcher and ran towards the abode of the Gandharvas and hid it there securely.

Meanwhile, in heaven, the gods came to know about the theft and were outraged. Unable to find a solution, the gods approached Goddess Saraswati for guidance. The goddess of knowledge listened to their concerns, and said, "Don't worry. I will get back the potion."

Goddess Saraswati disguised herself as a young maiden and carried her veena to where the Gandharvas lived. Once there, she began playing her divine music.

The air was filled with mellow tunes, and the Gandharvas were drawn to the music in no time. After some time the music suddenly stopped.

Vishvavasu asked the maiden, "Why did you stop playing? Could you please play again? Maybe you can teach us as well?"

The maiden said, "I would be delighted to teach you but I have one condition."

Thrilled at the idea of learning music, the Gandharvas cheerfully agreed.

"I want you to return the potion that you stole from the gods. If you agree, I, Saraswati, will happily grant you the knowledge of music."

The Gandharvas gave her the pitcher and learnt music whole heartedly. They came to be known as celestial musicians.

Ganga Gets Cursed

One day, Maharishi Durvasa was coming to Swarga Lok. He was known for becoming angry quickly and putting a curse if someone annoyed him. While he was wandering around, a rush of wind blew off the only piece of cloth that he had on his body. Durvasa kept trying to wrap himself with the cloth to avoid being naked. Watching Durvasa's struggle, Ganga began to chuckle. When Maharishi Durvasa heard Ganga's laughter, he was enraged.

He said, "You are very disrespectful, Ganga. You are a dishonor to Swarga Lok. I curse you to live on Earth as a river."

Ganga was stunned. The devas were shocked too and politely said, "O Maharishi, please pardon Ganga for her childlike behavior?"

"My curse cannot be repealed. But she can return to Swarga Lok when her water gets polluted," replied Durvasa.

Ganga Reaches Earth

Bhagirath, a former king and now a rishi, did great penance and prayed to Lord Shiva to relieve his ancestors from their curse. Due to a curse put on them, his ancestors' souls could never ascend to heaven. With his vigor and righteousness, Bhagirath impressed Lord Shiva.

Lord Shiva appeared before him and gave him a boon, "Dear Bhagirath, rise. I know your wish. I will fulfill it."

Delighted and overwhelmed, Bhagirath thanked Lord Shiva. The three-eyed god then asked Ganga to come down to Earth from heaven. He unfolded his hair across the sky, so Ganga would not flood Earth. The lord caught her in his hair and moved till she reached Earth. Slowly and steadily, he released Ganga from his entangled hair.

While following Bhagirath, Ganga thought of having some fun. She flowed inside the ashram of Rishi Janu and flooded the entire place. Rishi Janu was swiftly shaken from his penance. To punish Ganga, he swallowed her waters. Ganga panicked.

Trapped inside walls, Ganga begged, "Rishi Janu! Please forgive me for my careless act."

When Bhagirath realised what had happened, he ran to Sage Janu and cried, "O great Rishi, please forgive Ganga and release her. She is the only way through which my ancestors will reach heaven. I beg you."

Rishi Janu smiled and released the river.

Finally, Bhagirath reached the dry ocean bed with Ganga. The goddess then flowed over the ashes of the sons of Sagara and lifting them from their curse, sent them to heaven. Overwhelmed, Bhagirath once again thanked Lord Shiva for helping him.

Ganga and Shantanu

One day, King Shantanu went hunting and saw Goddess Ganga strolling around the river. He instantly fell in love with her and without hesitation asked her to marry him.

Ganga replied, "I will marry you but on one condition. You will never question me about my actions. If you do, I will leave you."

Shantanu assured her that he would never ask her for any clarification. Soon after they were married.

In time, they welcomed their first son. King Shantanu was overwhelmed with happiness. But it did not last long. Hours later, he saw Ganga going towards the river with their son. Curious, he followed her and was shocked to see Ganga drowning their son. Bound by his promise, he kept quiet. In similar manner, Ganga drowned their seven newborn sons. King Shantanu was filled with great sorrow.

When Ganga gave birth to their eighth son, King Shantanu broke his vow and asked her the reason behind drowning their children.

Ganga revealed a story from the past and said, "I have drowned the children to fulfill the curses upon them and us by Lord Brahma and Sage Vashishtha in our past lives."

Since, King Shantanu had spoken, Ganga left him. She took their eighth son to raise him. She promised to return him when the time was right.

Sixteen years later, Ganga came with their son, Devavrat, as she had promised. King Shantanu was delighted to meet his son.

Goddess Lakshmi Chooses Her Husband

For Goddess Lakshmi's Swayamwara, who had appeared during the churning of the ocean, all devas and asuras including Lord Vishnu, appeared. Goddess Lakshmi specifically studied Lord Vishnu with his sparkling eyes and mischievous smile. She smiled and placed the garland around his neck, choosing him as her husband.

The gods celebrated the marriage of Goddess Lakshmi and Lord Vishnu. She was goddess supreme, who had manifested herself as Lakshmi to become Lord Vishnu's wife – his power and strength.

Vaishno Devi

An adorable girl, Vaishnavi, was born in the family of Ratankar. Since her childhood, she displayed a thirst for knowledge. In time, Vaishnavi learned the art of meditation and looked into her inner self. She went deep into the woods to do *tapasya*.

Admiration for Vaishnavi spread far and wide, and soon people began to visit her ashram to seek her blessings. Once, Maha Yogi Guru Goraksh Nath Ji had a vision of an episode between Lord Rama and Vaishnavi. He was curious to know if she has been successful in attaining spirituality or not. So, he asked his disciple, "Bhairon Nath! I want you to find out the truth about Vaishnavi."

Once there, he instead got smitten by Vishanvi's extraordinary beauty. Bhairon Nath also noticed that she was always surrounded by langoors, a vicious lion, and carried bow and arrows. Captivated, Bhairon Nath began pestering her to marry him.

Once, a devotee of Vaishnavi, Mata Sridhar, organized a *bhandara* where the entire village was invited. Maha Yogi Goraksh Nath Ji along with his disciples came too. At the venue, Bhairon Nath tried to grab Vaishnavi and asked her to be his wife. She dodged him and escaped into the mountains to continue her *tapasya*. However, Bhairon continued to follow her.

When it got out of hand, Vaishnavi beheaded Bhairon just outside the mouth of a cave. Bhairon met his fate, and his detached head fell at the nearby hilltop. Upon his death, Bhairon Nath realized his mistake.

He prayed to the deity, "O Vaishno Devi! Please forgive me for my grave mistake."

The goddess listened to his prayer and had mercy on him.

Vaishno Devi and Shree Ram

Lord Rama visited Vaishnavi during his exile, and she immediately recognized him as an incarnation of Lord Vishnu.

She said, "My Lord, accept my marriage proposal."

Lord Rama replied, "Vaishnavi, this is not the right time, but I will revisit. If you recognize me, I will fulfill your wish."

Keeping his promise, Lord Rama visited Vaishnavi again but this time he was disguised as an old man. Vaishnavi was unable to recognize him. When she learnt who the old man was, she broke down. Rama consoled her and said, "This is not your time. It will eventually come in *Kalyug* when I am in the avatar of Kalki."

Sita's Marriage

One day, when the sun was shining brightly, King Janak of Mithila was working in the fields. As he thought of going back, he heard a coo. When he followed the voice, he saw a little baby girl staring back at him with a sweet smile on her face.

He asked her, "Sweet girl. Where did you come from?"

No one was around, except the two of them. The girl kept quiet.

Overjoyed, Janak considered her a gift from Goddess Earth and took the girl with him. He named her Sita.

Years passed by. One day, Sita was playing with her sisters and accidentally lifted the table over which the Shiv Dhanush was kept. This divine bow was so heavy that no one could even move it an inch. Janak, who was in the room, was stunned. It was then that he decided that he must find a groom equivalent to Sita's power.

Years passed, King Janak organized a swayamwar for his daughter, Sita. He invited worthy kings and princes and announced that whosoever wishes to marry Sita must lift the mighty Shiv Dhanush.

Many princes and kings tried but it was only Lord Rama who accomplished the impossible task. He lifted the Shiv Dhanush! But just as he tried to string it, it broke with a thunderous sound.

As everyone was celebrating, Lord Parshurama came to the palace demanding to know who had broken the Shiv Dhanush. Rama humbly replied that it was he. Furious Parashurama wanted to fight him. But Janak intervened and calmed down Parshurama. The latter learned what had happened at the palace and blessed the couple, realizing their true identity.

Durga

Mahishasura, the king of asuras, performed rigorous penance to appease Lord Brahma. Pleased with his austerities, Brahma finally appeared before him and said, "Ask me for a boon."

Mahishasura said, "Lord Brahma, if I must die, let it be at the hands of a woman."

Brahma granted him the boon and disappeared. Mahishasura was ecstatic at becoming immortal. He considered women weak and helpless without the ability to kill him. In no time, he gathered his army and attacked Amaravati, deva's kingdom.

Indra, the king of devas, challenged Mahishasura and hurled his thunderbolt at him. The thunderbolt did not affect Mahishasura and he defeated Indra with ease. The devas fled the battlefield and lived in exile.

Creation of Goddess Durga

Mahishasura conquered all that lived in no time. He ordered everyone to worship him as the supreme god. The asuras under his reign tortured and killed the saints and devotees who worshipped the devas.

Unable to bear the cruelties of the asuras, the devas sought help in Lord Shiva and went to Kailash mountain. Hearing their pleas, bright rays of light came from Shiva, Vishnu, Indra, Brahma and other devas' wrathful faces. The lights united and formed a female form with ten arms. She was Goddess Durga.

Filled with hope, the devas said, "Devi! You are the beginning of all the worlds, the inner force and the foundation of all strength. You are Durga! Please help us! Destroy Mahishasura and protect everyone."

The goddess was ready to meet Mahisasura. Then, loaded with weapons given to her by all the gods, she went forth to meet the invincible Mahishasura.

Durga Fights Mahisha's Army

Charging towards the army of the asuras, riding a lion and loaded with celestial weapons, Durga emitted a blood-curdling roar — ready to seek out and destroy Mahishasura. As Durga marched forward, the world shivered, the sky grew dark and the sea went still. The sight made Mahishasura miss a heartbeat. He rushed out of his palace and saw the goddess shaking all the three lokas.

Seeing his arrogant face, Durga said, "I have come to fulfil Brahma's boon. You wanted to die at the hands of a woman, didn't you? Come and fight me."

Mahishasura replied, "O, a woman will fight me? I have defeated Indra and the other devas. Who are you? You are beautiful; you should marry me."

Durga shouted in anger, "You foolish evil! Come fight me and marry your death!"

Outraged, Mahishasura called his army and ordered them to kill Durga. As commanded, the asuras hurled various weapons at her. Without flinching, Durga summoned her army.

As she breathed, thousands of battalions came into being with her power. Soon, the sky was filled with strong weapons and spears were being showered from both sides. Durga's army followed her and they destroyed thousands of asuras.

Burning with rage, Mahishasura said, "I will crush this monstrous woman and her army."

Durga Kills Mahisha

Infuriated, Mahishasura took the form of a buffalo, charged forth, snorting and bawling. He trampled Durga's army and pounded them with his tail, killing all that came in his way.

Durga looked at the sight, and enraged, she flung a strap at the buffalo. Mahishasura stopped himself and transformed into a lion, and attacked the Devi. With her trident, Durga chopped off the lion's head. However, Mahishasura again rose in his actual form and charged. Then, he became an elephant and towed at Durga's mount with his trunk.

Durga slashed off the trunk with her sword. Mahishasura again appeared as a buffalo and rushed forward with rage and said, "No one can kill me. I am invincible!"

Looking at him, Durga said, "You fool! Soon the devas will roar in triumph at the very place where you will be slain."

Mahishasura charged at her in anger once again, but Durga leapt upon him and pinned him down. He struggled to free himself as half of his body emerged from the mouth of the buffalo. Negating his efforts, Durga raised her sword and struck off his head, killing the great asura. As his body lay on the ground, the asura army too perished.

Seeing the victorious Durga, the devas cheered, "Durga, destroyer of evil! We are thankful to you. Continue to protect us, devi."

Durga replied, "Whenever you need me, I will come."

Ambika Gets A Marriage Proposal

In time, the evil asuras returned and attacked heaven once again. Shumbha, the asura's lord, drove out the devas including Indra and took control over everything. Chanda and Munda, commanders of Shumbha, followed the devas to find out where they would go.

The devas went to Mount Himavat and prayed to Goddess Durga, "Devi! Protector of the virtuous and the light of the universe, overthrow Shumbha and his evil army to restore uprightness."

Goddess Durga, in the form of Ambika, appeared at Himavat. Chanda and Munda reached there too but seeing Ambika they did not bother about the devas.

Stunned by Ambika's beauty, both Chanda and Munda thought she was fit to be married to their master. So, they approached her and said, "Shumbha, the great lord of the three worlds, who retains incomparable fortune, wants to marry you."

Ambika said, "It's not that easy. I am bound by a vow that I had taken a long time ago. I will only marry the man who can defeat me in battle and humble my pride."

Aggravated, Chanda and Munda returned to their master to inform him of Ambika's stubbornness and ridiculous vow.

Death of Dhumraochana

Shumbha agrees to fulfill Ambika's wish for a battle. He turned to Dhumraochana, one of his commanders and ordered him to bring Ambika to his palace by force and to kill whosoever intervenes as her saviour.

Dhumraochana met Ambika and said, "O woman! Come with us. Our great lord Shumbha is waiting for you. If you don't come by yourself, I will have to take you by force."

Pretending to be scared, Ambika replied, "I must fight him."

Hearing this, Dhumraochana rushed at her with his sword. Ambika meanwhile, emitted a sound hmm with absolute contempt for the asura, and at once, he turned to ashes.

Chanda Munda

Watching their commander turn to ashes, the asuras started to flee.

Chanda and Munda tried stopping them, "We have been ordered to capture this maleficent woman. We will not give up. She is alone and we are many."

Ambika, seated on a lion, was surrounded by the asuras. Looking at them, she scowled, and from her forehead came a light, which created Goddess Kali. Mighty Kali stormed at the asuras and crumpled them to death.

Chanda hurried towards Kali grumbling about feeding her to the vultures. But instead he was seized by his hair and beheaded instantly by Kali. Minutes later, his brother, Munda met the same fate.

Smiling at Kali, Ambika said, "Since, you have killed Chanda and Munda, you will be known Chamundi."

Raktabeej

Shumbha went to fight Ambika himself when he heard about the death of his commanders—Chanda and Munda. As the asuras encircled both Ambika and Kali, from the inner forces of various gods rose other shaktis — out of Brahma emerged Brahmani, out of Maheshwara came Maheshwari, out of Vishnu, Vaishnavi, out of Ambika appeared Chandika. Soon the sky was filled with thousands of shaktis. The Shaktis fought the asuras and made them flee.

From among them, Asura Raktabeej screamed, "Shame on you all! Running from women! Come back and fight."

When Raktabeej rushed forward to fight, Indra's Shakti struck him with her thunderbolt and he died. As his blood touched the ground, out of it many more Raktabeej came to life. In no time, the battleground was crammed with thousands of Raktabeejs fighting the Shaktis.

As Raktabeejs, kept rising, Chandika turned to Kali, "Chamundi, we have to stop their blood from falling to the ground, only then we can defeat them."

Kali replied, "I will take care of it. Their blood won't stain the earth ever again."

As the Shaktis fought the Raktabeejs, Kali intervened collecting all the blood in a vessel and soon, thousands of Raktabeejs were wiped out. Frantic, Raktabeej hurried towards Chandika who struck him and Kali prevented his blood from falling to the earth. Raktabeej fell dead, and the devas cheered.

Nishumba Gets Killed

When Shumbha and his brother Nishumbha head about this incident, they were shocked and wondered how the mighty asuras were defeated by a woman.

Confidently, Nishumbha said, "Brother, don't worry. I will deal with her."

Shumbha replied, "Only you are capable of killing her, Nishumbha."

Nishumbha marched with his army to finally put an end to Chandika. In time, the evil asura army met Chandika and surrounded her from all sides. Weapons were hurled at her from all sides. Nishumbha too attacked her with everything he had got. Yet, even the most powerful asura was no match to Chandika. He too lost his life at her hands. Whatever was left of his army, fled from the scene.

Overwhelmed and angered to his see his dear brother butchered and his asura army slaughtered mercilessly, Shumbha at last went to meet Durga.

He said, "There is no praise in your victory, Durga. You have had others' help by which you defeated my army. Now, I will put an end to you!"

Durga replied, "You fool! All the goddesses that you see are my powers, my different forms."

Astonished, Shumbha watched as all Shaktis merged into Durga, and only Ambika remained.

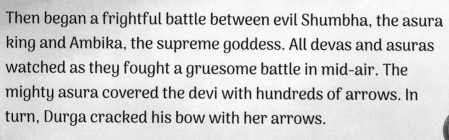

Then began a frightful battle between evil Shumbha, the asura king and Ambika, the supreme goddess. All devas and asuras watched as they fought a gruesome battle in mid-air. The mighty asura covered the devi with hundreds of arrows. In turn, Durga cracked his bow with her arrows.

Without a charioteer, with his stallions slain and bow broken, the asura grabbed his dreadful mace, ready to kill. Ambika, with her sharp arrows, split the mace. Shumbha then raised his fist on the heart of the devi, but she struck him on his chest with her palm. The wounded asura fell on earth with a resonating thump.

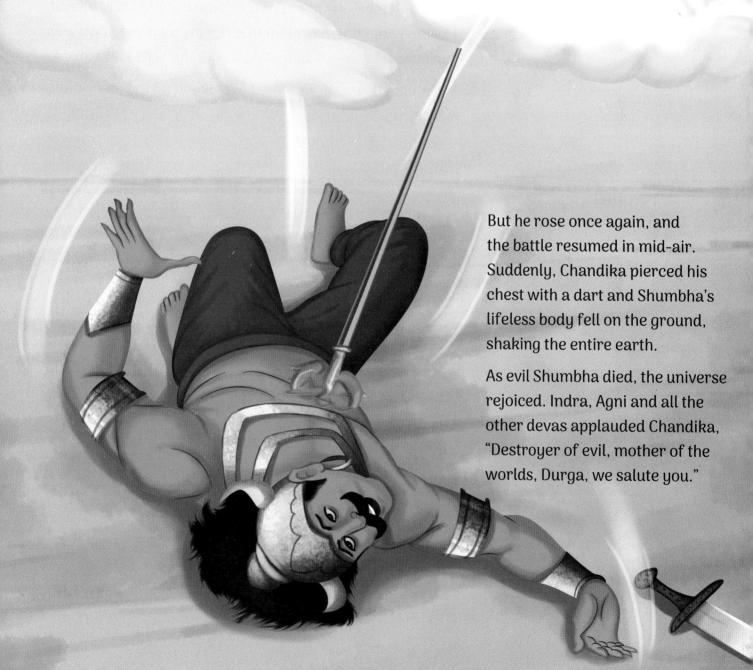

But he rose once again, and the battle resumed in mid-air. Suddenly, Chandika pierced his chest with a dart and Shumbha's lifeless body fell on the ground, shaking the entire earth.

As evil Shumbha died, the universe rejoiced. Indra, Agni and all the other devas applauded Chandika, "Destroyer of evil, mother of the worlds, Durga, we salute you."

Heramba

One day Goddess Parvati asked Nandi to guard the palace gates at Mount Kailash while she took her bath. Soon Lord Shiva arrived and commanded Nandi to step aside. Unable to disobey his supreme lord, Nandi let him pass. Goddess Parvati was hurt and angry at Nandi's behavior.

She rubbed off some turmeric paste from her body and made an idol of a boy. She then breathed life into the idol. When the boy opened his eyes, she said, "You are my son, Heramba. I am your mother and you must always remain loyal to me."

She then instructed Heramba to guard the palace gates and not let anyone come inside. Soon Lord Shiva returned. Heramba did not allow him to enter inside. Lord Shiva was furious and asked Nandi to deal with the arrogant kid.

Heramba, however, defeated Nandi and all the other Ganas with ease.

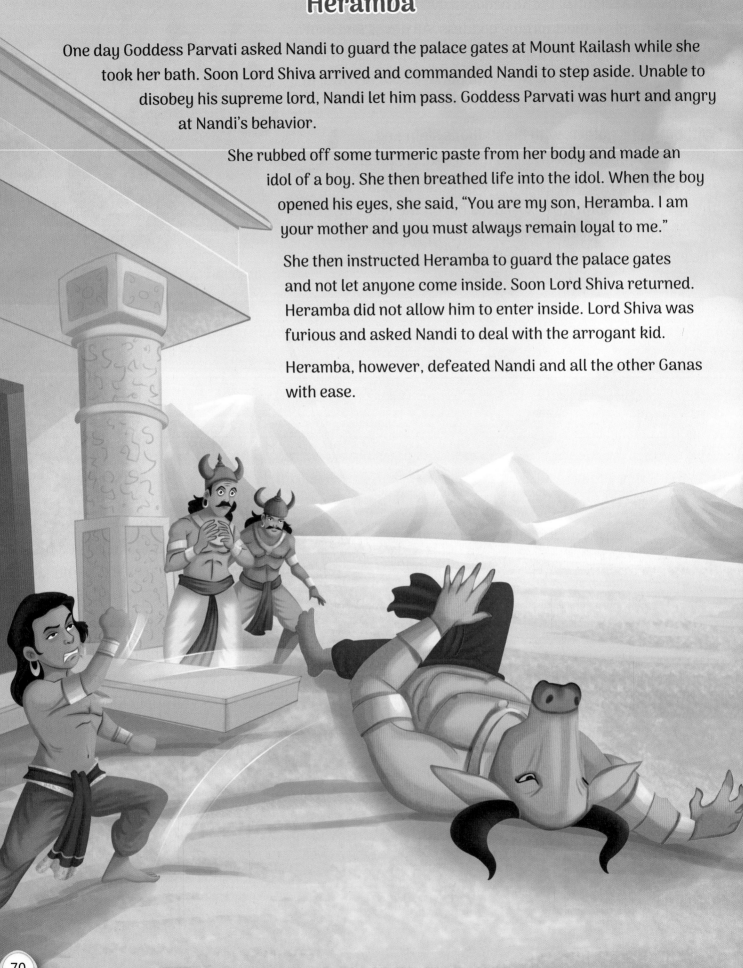

Fearing Lord Shiva's anger, all the gods came to pacify him. They assured him that they will deal with Heramba. But Heramba refused to listen to any argument. Indra and the other gods attacked Heramba but he defeated all of them. Then, Lord Shiva summoned his elder son Kartikeya and ordered him to defeat Heramba. Kartikeya was reluctant to harm his own brother but he obeyed his father.

Kartikeya challenged Heramba to a duel. After a prolonged battle, Heramba knocked Kartikeya unconscious. Lord Shiva's fury knew no bounds seeing the unconscious body of his son. Wrathful, he chopped off Heramba's head.

When Goddess Parvati found out about the death of her son, she roared with anger, "You gods have killed my innocent child who was simply obeying his mother's command. The whole universe will pay for killing my son."

Ganesha

The gods rushed to Lord Shiva and asked him to prevent the annihilation of the entire universe. Lord Shiva asked Lord Vishnu to bring the head of a dead animal. Lord Vishnu returned with the head of a baby elephant. Lord Shiva attached that elephant head to Heramba's body and chanted the *Mahamritunjaya* Mantra to bring him back to life.

When Heramba revived, Lord Shiva blessed him saying, "Henceforth you will be known as Ganesha, the head of all my ganas. People will worship you first before starting any auspicious work. You shall also be known as the god of wisdom and knowledge."

Ganesha bowed before his father humbly. The other gods also blessed Ganesha. Goddess Parvati's anger subsided.

Ganesha and the Cat

One day, Ganesha was playing with his friends. He spotted a cat and decided to tease it for fun. He held the cat by its tail and teased it until the poor animal cried in pain. The cat wriggled to set itself free and fell on the ground. Ganesha tried to get hold of the cat again but it run away.

Ganesha bid farewell to his friends and went back home. He went to his mother Parvati and said, "Mother, I am hungry."

When Goddess Parvati arrived with the food, Ganesha spotted bruises on her body. He was worried and asked, "Who gave you those bruises?"

She said, "You did. I wanted to play with you so I disguised myself as a cat."

Ganesha was ashamed of his behavior. He pledged to never hurt an innocent creature and hugged his mother.

Ganesha and Kuber

Kubera, the god of wealth and prosperity was extremely proud of his wealth. He built a lavish palace and organized a grand feast to celebrate the occasion. He invited the sages and all other gods. Finally, he arrived at Mount Kailash to invite Lord Shiva to the feast.

Aware of his intentions, Lord Shiva said, "I won't be able to attend the feast but take my son Ganesha with you. He loves to eat delicacies."

Lord Kubera replied, "Don't worry! Ganesha will remember my grand feast forever."

Lord Ganesha arrived at the palace of Lord Kubera. At the feast, he saw Kubera boasting about his riches and lavish lifestyle. He decided to teach Kubera a lesson in humility. In time the food was served. Ganesha devoured all the food that was served to him in no time and demanded for more.

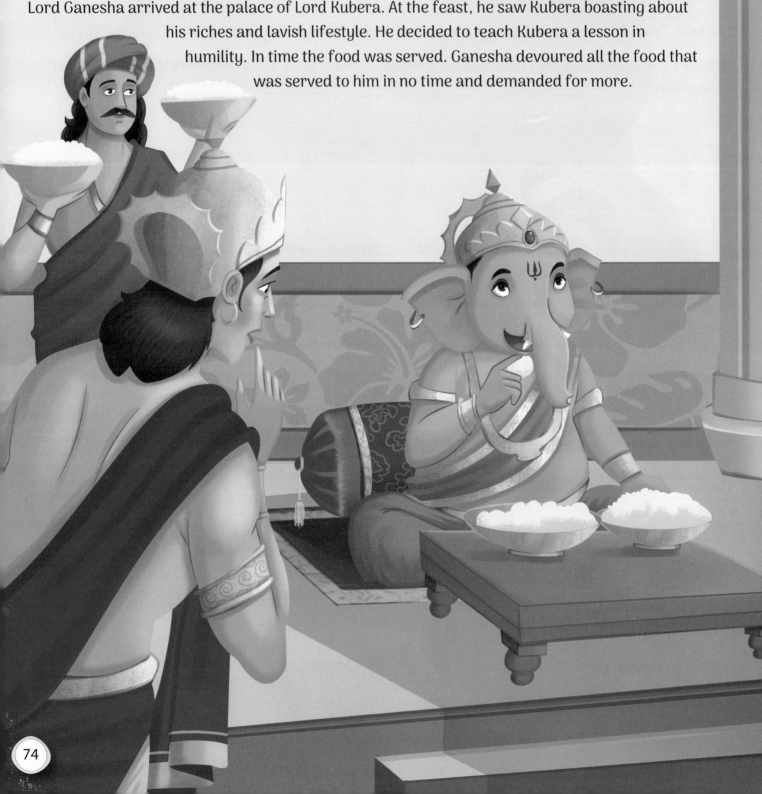

Ganesha, however, gobbled all the food that was served to him and kept demanding more. The servants rushed to Kubera and said, "Lord Ganesha has eaten all the food we had prepared for the feast. There is nothing left in the kitchen. We can't serve anything to the other guests."

Meanwhile, Ganesha had started eating the utensils. Seeing Kubera, he warned him, "If you don't serve me more food, I will eat you as well."

Kubera was terrified and ran to Lord Shiva. He apologized for his behavior and asked him to suggest a way to satiate Ganesha's hunger.

Lord Shiva suggested, "Serve Ganesha a bowl of rice with love and humility."

Lord Kubera went back to his palace. He, filled with humility, served a bowl of rice to Ganesha. Ganesha ate the rice and said, "I am done. I can't eat anymore."

Kubera was humbled by this incident. He apologized to everyone and promised never to brag about his riches.

Ganesha Curses the Moon

Ganesha was returning home after his dinner at Kubera's palace. Since, he had eaten a lot of food, his mount, the mouse, was unable to bear his weight. The mouse lost his balance and Ganesha fell down.

The moon god, who saw everything, burst out laughing and taunted Ganesha, "Poor mouse couldn't bear the weight of a fat kid."

Ganesha became angry and cursed the moon, "You have made fun of my anguish and so, you will also lose your shine and become invisible."

The moon begged Ganesha for forgiveness. Ganesha felt remorse on losing his temper and said, "I cannot reverse the curse but I will reduce its power. You will lose your shine gradually and become invisible for one day in a month before regaining your shine gradually."

From that day , the phases of the moon came into being.

Ekdant

One day, Lord Shiva wanted to meditate in peace and instructed his son Ganesha to not let anyone disturb him. Suddenly, Sage Parshuram arrived at Mount Kailash to meet Lord Shiva.

However, Ganesha, still a child, blocked his path and said, "Father is meditating and I can't let you meet him."

Parshuram lost his temper. A fight broke out between them. After a prolonged fight, Parshuram threw his Parshu at Ganesha. Since the Parshu belonged to Lord Shiva, Ganesha honored it by taking its blow on his left tusk. The weapon chopped off Ganesha's tusk and he fell on the ground howling in pain.

Goddess Parvati came running to the spot. On seeing Ganesha's condition, she was furious. Seeing her, Parshuram realized his mistake. He then blessed Ganesha and gave him a new name, 'Ekdant'.

Ganesha and Ravana

The demon king Ravana, ruler of Lanka, was a great devotee of Lord Shiva. He had performed severe penances for years to appease Lord Shiva.

One day, he came to Mount Kailash and pleaded with Lord Shiva, "Please grant me a boon that my city, Lanka, will never get destroyed."

Impressed by his devotion, Lord Shiva gave him an Aathma Lingam and said, "Mount this in Lanka and your kingdom will be impregnable. But you have to carry this back holding it in your hands. Remember, not to put it down before you reach Lanka. If you do so it will take root and never move."

Ravana agreed to the condition and holding the Aathma Lingam started his journey towards Lanka on foot.

However, the gods in heaven felt that Ravana will become all the more powerful. Together, they approached Lord Ganesha and asked him to help.

So, Lord Ganesha filled Ravana's stomach with water. Ravana gradually realized that he had to address nature's call. He was in a dilemma. It was at this time that Ganesha came disguised as a village kid.

Seeing the kid, Ravana said, "Hold this Lingam for me and don't put it down. I will return soon."

The child agreed but on a condition. He said, "When I get tired, I will call you thrice. If you don't appear, I will put the Lingam on the ground and go my way."

Ravana agreed to the condition and handed over the Lingam to the kid. As planned, Lord Ganesha called for Ravana three times the moment he was out of sight. When Ravana did not return, he placed the Lingam on the ground and vanished.

Ravana was devastated when he came back. He tried to lift the Aathma Lingam but it was all in vain.

Origin of River Kaveri

In ancient days, southern India had no major river. This resulted in severe droughts and people suffered due to it. Seeing their misery, Rishi Agastya requested Lord Shiva to help the people.

Then, Lord Shiva poured a little bit of Ganges water into his Kamandalu and said, "Oh respected one! Take this water with you. Pour it at an apt place which will lead to the creation of a mighty river."

Rishi Agastya thanked Lord Shiva and left Kailash. During his journey, the sage stopped near Koorg mountains. It was then that he saw Ganesha playing with his mouse nearby. He gave the Kamandalu to Ganesha and said, "Hold this Kamandalu for me for some time. I need to rest and meditate."

Ganesha agreed to help the wise sage.

After a while, Ganesha was tired of waiting for the rishi and he started looking for him to wake up.

Ganesha, unable to wait anymore, transformed himself into a crow and tipped the Kamandalu. Water trickled out it. Soon the trickle changed into a torrent and a mighty river began to flow from that very spot.

The sound of rushing water woke up Rishi Agastya. Ganesha spoke humbly to the sage, saying, "I am sorry that I spilled the water from your Kamandalu but I thought that it is the right spot for the origin of the river."

Rishi Agastya smiled and said, "Do not apologise. You have brought water to this barren land. I shall name this river, Kaveri."

Lord Ganesha's Marriage

One day, Lord Shiva and Goddess Parvati called their sons, Lord Ganesha and Lord Kartikeya and said, "Dear sons! It's about time that you two should get married. However, both of you are equal for us and we are unable to decide whose marriage should take place first. Hence we have decided to hold a competition. Whoever completes three revolutions of the universe shall be declared the winner and will get married first."

Both Lord Ganesha and Lord Kartikeya agreed to compete. Lord Kartikeya swiftly mounted his peacock and began his journey to travel across the universe.

Lord Ganesha knew that he would not be able to compete with his brother riding on his mouse so he fell back on his knowledge and wisdom. He folded his hands and circled around his parents three times.

Goddess Parvati asked him, "Ganesha, your brother is already on his way. Why aren't you following him?"

Ganesha smiled and replied, "I have won the competition, mother. Now, make preparations for my marriage."

Goddess Parvati was perplexed and said, "How have you won the competition? You have not even begun the race yet."

Lord Ganesha smiled and confidently replied, "According to the holy Vedas, parents are their children's entire universe. I have completed three revolutions around the universe when I circled three times around you, my parents."

Lord Shiva and Goddess Parvati were pleased with Lord Ganesha and declared him the winner. Soon Lord Ganesha was married to Riddhi and Siddhi.

It was some time before Lord Kartikeya returned, only to find his brother married.

Ganesha Writes *Mahabharata*

Sage Ved Vyasa wished to write *Mahabharata* and decided to find a writer who could write the verses as he recited them. He approached Lord Ganesha and asked for his assistance.

Lord Ganesha said, "I am ready to do it but you must fulfill one condition. You must dictate the entire epic in one go. If you stop in between, I will stop writing it and will return to my abode."

Sage Ved Vyasa agreed to Lord Ganesha's condition and replied, "I too have a condition. You must understand the verses completely before you write them."

Lord Ganesha agreed and they started writing the epic. Sage Ved Vyasa deliberately used tough phrases whenever he needed a breather from narrating the stories. Lord Ganesha took a break to understand them, allowing Ved Vyasa to compose his thoughts. It was in this manner that the epic was composed.

The Red Fruit

Anjaneya was the son of the mighty monkey king, Kesari, and his wife Anjana. He was an incarnation of Lord Shiva and was born due to the blessings of Vayu, the wind god. Hence, he inherited supernatural powers. He was also known as Vayuputra or the son of Lord Vayu.

One day, Anjaneya mistook the sun for a ripe red fruit. He leapt in the air and was about to eat it when, Lord Surya, the sun god, got worried and shouted, "Help!"

Lord Indra rushed out on his elephant to stop Anjaneya from harming the sun. He tried to reason with him, but the young child was determined to eat the sun.

Finally, Lord Indra had to throw his Vajra to stop Anjaneya. The thunderbolt hit him on his chin and knocked him unconscious as he went crashing towards earth. Lord Vayu, his father, caught the boy and went inside a cave.

Lord Vayu was furious and stopped the flow of air on earth. Every creature began to suffocate. The gods panicked and reached the cave to placate Lord Vayu.

Lord Brahma healed Anjaneya's injuries. The child revived. Lord Brahma blessed him, "No weapon will ever be able to harm you." Lord Indra too blessed Anjaneya, "I give you the gift of immortality." He then said, "Due to your pronounced chin you will be known as 'Hanuman'. You will be a 'chiranjeevi', or one with an extraordinarily long life."

The other gods too blessed Hanuman with several powers, including that of knowledge and wisdom, extraordinary strength and the ability to change shape and size. Lord Vayu thanked the gods and revived the airflow on earth.

Hanuman Gets a Curse

Hanuman loved to play pranks and did not listen to the advice of his parents. He was also unable to control his incredible strength and supernatural powers. He disturbed the sages meditating in the forest and damaged their ashrams for his amusement. The sages had warned Hanuman several times, but he paid no attention to their requests.

One day, Hanuman reached an ashram, uprooted a tree and threw it away. The sages lost their patience. One of the sages bellowed, "I curse you that you will forget all your powers!" But a compassionate sage said, "You will remember your powers once someone reminds you of them."

And so, Hanuman forgot about his powers and became a humble child. He went back home and never disturbed the sages again.

A Lesson by Lord Surya

One day, Hanuman approached Lord Surya, bowed before him humbly and said, "Lord, I wish to acquire the knowledge and wisdom of our holy scriptures. I have come here to request you to become my teacher."

Lord Surya was impressed by Hanuman's gentle nature. He replied, "I would love to teach you. However, I can't stop at one place; I am constantly moving."

Hanuman bowed and said, "My Lord, I will also travel alongside and fly backwards. This way, you won't have to stop and I can still take my lessons."

Lord Surya gladly agreed to this proposal and started teaching Hanuman. When Hanuman completed his studies, he asked Lord Surya about his gurudakshina or fees. Lord Surya said, "Hanuman, I want you to help my son Sugreev, the monkey prince of Kishkinda. He has lost his kingdom."

Hanuman promised to help Sugreev and went to his kingdom.

Hanuman Meets Ram

Hanuman went to the Rishiyamukh mountain, where Sugreev lived in exile. The monkey prince welcomed him and made him his chief advisor.

One day, Hanuman saw two young men roaming in the forest. Suspicious, he transformed himself into a beggar and sat under a tree. The strangers approached him. One of them said, "My name is Ram and this is my brother Lakshman. We are searching for my wife Sita, who has been... Wait, why are you begging in the forest while wearing a diamond necklace? Who are you?"

Hanuman was surprised and replied, "You can see my invisible necklace? My mother had told me that only my true master will be able to spot it. I have been waiting for you my whole life! My name is Hanuman."

Hanuman then appeared in his true form. He then invited Lord Ram and Lakshman to meet Sugreev.

Hanuman Crosses the Ocean

After Sugreev became the king of the Vanaras, he sent teams in every direction to find Mother Sita. Lord Ram gave his ring to Hanuman and said, "Give it to Sita. She will trust your message when she sees this."

Hanuman and a team of Vanaras reached the ocean. Then, the wise bear Jambvant reminded Hanuman of his powers, and the curse of the sage was broken. Hanuman leapt into the air and began flying towards Lanka.

Soon, the serpent goddess, Sursa, stopped Hanuman and challenged him to enter her open mouth. Hanuman expanded in size, but Sursa enlarged her mouth accordingly. Suddenly, Hanuman reduced himself to his original size, entered Sursa's mouth and came out quickly.

He bowed before Sursa and said, "I have fulfilled your challenge. Now, let me go." Impressed by Hanuman's wit, she blessed him and wished him success in his mission.

Hanuman resumed his journey. He was about to reach the shores of Lanka when he realized that he wasn't able to fly ahead. When he looked below, he saw that his shadow had been captured by Simhika, a sea-demon who caught the shadows of her prey and then ate them alive. Before Hanuman could free himself, she leapt out of the sea and swallowed him whole. As soon as Hanuman reached her belly, he started tearing her from the inside using his nails and freed himself.

Finally, Hanuman reached the golden city of Lanka. When he tried to enter Lanka, he was stopped by Lankini, the powerful gatekeeper of Lanka. When she tried to attack Hanuman, he struck her gently, but Lankini instantly fell to the ground.

She then bowed before him and said, "Lord Brahma had predicted that the demise of Ravan and his army would begin when a monkey will hit me. That time has come. You can enter Lanka."

Adventure in Ashok Vatika

Hanuman was searching for Mother Sita in the city of Lanka when he heard someone chanting Lord Vishnu's name. He saw Vibhishan, the youngest brother of asura king Ravan, worshipping Lord Vishnu's idol. So, Hanuman sought his help. Vibhishan directed him to Ashok Vatika.

Hanuman spotted divine Sita sitting alone under a tree. He hid behind some branches and waited till the female demons guarding Sita left her alone. Meanwhile, he quietly dropped Ram's ring in her lap.

Sita immediately recognised her husband's ring and became anxious. Hanuman appeared in front of her and respectfully said, "Mother, my name is Hanuman. I am the messenger of your husband and my master Shree Ram."

Sita was elated to see Hanuman and asked about her husband's well-being.

Hanuman narrated Ram's adventures and offered to take Sita back to her husband.

Sita firmly said, "I cannot come with you, Hanuman. Shree Ram must defeat Ravan and take me back with him with the dignity befitting a queen. Tell him that I am waiting for the day when I will be united with him."

Sita gave Hanuman some of her jewelry and said, "Give this to Shree Ram. Seeing these, he will believe that your quest was successful."

After bidding farewell to Mother Sita, Hanuman started uprooting trees in the royal garden and wreaked havoc on the guards. Ravan was furious. He sent his son Akshay Kumar to kill Hanuman. However, Hanuman killed him.

Finally, Ravan's oldest and mightiest son, Meghnath offered to capture Hanuman. He attacked Hanuman with the supreme weapon, Brahmastra. To honor Lord Brahma, Hanuman bowed before the weapon and allowed himself to be captured.

Hanuman Burns Lanka

Meghnath tied Hanuman in chains and presented him in the royal court. When Ravan did not offer him a place to sit, Hanuman extended his tail and looped it many times to create a seat which was higher than Ravan's throne.

Ravan roared with anger, "Who are you? How dare you enter Lanka and kill my beloved son?"

Hanuman replied, "My name is Hanuman! I am a messenger of Shree Ram. I have come here to warn you, if you don't release Mother Sita, your demise is inevitable."

Ravan became furious hearing Hanuman's threat and ordered his men to kill him.

Vibhishan cautioned Ravan and said, "Brother! We mustn't kill a messenger. He was only delivering his master's message." Ravan contemplated for a moment and said, "Fine! Don't kill him. Since he is so proud of his tail, set it on fire."

As per Ravan's order, Hanuman's tail was set ablaze. Hanuman decided to teach Ravan a lesson. He broke his shackles with ease. Then, he jumped from one building to another, setting Lanka on fire.

Soon the entire city was in flames. The residents fled from their houses and ran into the streets. The royal soldiers tried to catch Hanuman but failed. Hanuman spared only Ashok Vatika, where Mother Sita was kept prisoner.

After ensuring that Sita was unharmed, Hanuman leapt into the ocean and extinguished the fire on his tail. He then returned to his friends, waiting for him, on the other side of the ocean. They were eager to return to Lord Rama.

Hanuman Saves Lakshman

During the battle between Ram and Ravan's armies, Meghnath attacked Lakshman with his most powerful weapon—Shakti. Lakshman immediately fell unconscious. Upon Vibhishan's request, Sushena, the royal physician of Lanka, inspected Lakshman and said, "I need Sanjeevani Booti to heal him, a herb that grows on the Dronagiri mountain in the Himalayas. I must get it before sunrise."

Lord Ram requested Hanuman to bring the Sanjeevani Booti, as he was the only one capable of flying. Ravan sent the demon Kalanemi to stop Hanuman from coming back in time. Kalanemi disguised as a sage, set up a magical hermitage around a lake in the Himalayas and began chanting Lord Ram's name to lure Hanuman. Hanuman came to the hermitage to rest. Kalanemi welcomed him and suggested that he take a bath in the lake.

While Hanuman was taking a bath, he was attacked by a crocodile. When he killed the crocodile, an apsara emerged from within and said, "Thank you for freeing me from Sage Durvasa's curse. But beware of the sage who sent you here, he is an asura." Hanuman thanked her and returned to the hermitage.

Kalanemi was surprised to see Hanuman alive. Hanuman didn't wait and thrashed the asura before resuming his journey. When he reached the Dronagiri mountain, he couldn't identify the Sanjeevani Booti. So, he decided to uproot the mountain and brought the entire peak with him.

To everyone's relief, Hanuman returned before dawn. He placed the mountain on the ground. The physician applied the herb on Lakshman's wound. Everyone was elated when Lakshman opened his eyes. Lord Ram profusely thanked Hanuman for saving his brother's life.

Hanuman Proves His Devotion

After his return to Ayodhya and coronation, Lord Ram said, "Dear Hanuman, what can I offer you as reward?"

Hanuman replied, "My Lord! Being with you is my greatest reward."

Mother Sita offered Hanuman her pearl necklace. After taking the necklace with utmost respect, he broke it down to pieces. He then checked every single pearl and threw it away. Everybody was surprised by this behavior. When questioned, Hanuman calmly explained, "These pearls don't have my Lord Ram in them. So, I can't keep the necklace."

One of the courtiers mocked Hanuman and said, "Can you prove that you have Lord Ram inside yourself?"

Instantly, Hanuman tore open his chest and showed an image of Shree Ram and Mother Sita residing in it. Lord Ram immediately embraced Hanuman and said, "You have won me over with your devotion. I give myself to you as a gift."

Hanuman Meets Bheem

Bheem, one of the Pandava brothers, was once walking in the forest when he bumped into a frail monkey lying on the ground. He roared, "Move out of my way, you old monkey! I'm mighty Bheem, the son of Lord Vayu. I possess the strength of a hundred elephants."

The monkey smiled and said, "I believe you! But I am too old and weak. Why don't you lift my tail and move me aside to make way for yourself?"

But to his surprise, Bheem couldn't move it even a bit. He bowed and said, "My Lord! You can't be an ordinary monkey. Please reveal your true identity."

Hanuman regained his true form and embraced Bheem. He blessed him and said, "Dear brother, your strength has increased manifold with my embrace. You shall be victorious in the war to come."

Demons in Gokul

Kansa imprisoned Devaki, his sister, and her husband Vasudeva because her eighth son was destined to kill him. He was shocked to learn that Devaki's eighth son was living safely under foster care. He summoned a powerful demoness, Pootna and commanded her to kill all the infants in his kingdom.

Pootna turned herself into a beautiful woman and went from village to village, murdering babies. When she arrived at Gokul, she went to Nanda's house and picked up baby Krishna.

Pootna took Krishna to a deserted place and started breastfeeding him after applying poison on her breast. Soon, Pootna experienced excruciating pain in her breast. Krishna sucked the life out of her, and her lifeless body dropped on the ground.

When Kansa found out about Pootna's death, he summoned a demon named Trinavarta and commanded, "You must kill the infant responsible for Pootna's death!"

Trinavarta accepted the task and reached Gokul. He began spying on Krishna. Soon, he found Krishna unattended. Seizing the opportunity, he turned himself into a tornado, scooped away Krishna and rose high in the sky. He was elated. After a while, Trinavarta was unable to hold Krishna as his weight increased tremendously. He struggled to stay up in the sky. In this moment, Krishna began punching the demon's chest, killing him instantly.

Trinavarta crashed on the ground with a thud. Krishna was beside him, unharmed.

Krishna Lifts a Curse

Krishna loved to eat butter. He became known in his hometown for his mischiefs and his habit of breaking into houses with his friends to steal butter. Several women complained to Yashoda who refused to believe them.

However, one day, Yashoda caught Krishna and his friends stealing butter.

Yashoda tied Krishna to a heavy mortar to punish him. Krishna wanted to set himself free so he dragged himself and the mortar towards the river hoping one of his friends would untie him. However, he got stuck among two trees growing side by side. He uprooted the two trees and in turn liberated Nalakuvara and Manigriva, sons of Kubera, who were cursed to become trees. He too was free now.

Adventures in Vrindavan

Once, Aghasura the mighty serpent demon swore to kill Krishna to avenge the death of his siblings—Pootna and Bakasura. He went to the forest near Gokul, transformed into a giant snake and lay still with his mouth open.

The next day Krishna and his friends brought their cattle to graze in the forest when they saw a large cave resembling a huge serpent. Everybody decided to explore the cave. Krishna knew that his friends were in danger. He stepped inside Aghasura's mouth last and gradually increased his size. Aghasura soon was in immense pain and finally he choked to death.

Soon, Krishna and his friends stepped out of Aghasura's mouth safe and sound.

Kalia Nag, the giant serpent king, shifted to River Yamuna along with his family. The river's water became toxic due to their presence. One hot day, cattle rushed towards Yamuna to quench their thirst. The next moment, they fell down on the ground, dead.

Krishna dived into Yamuna to find the culprit. Kalia Nag spotted Krishna and spewed venom towards him from his multiple heads. Krishna dodged the venom and struck several powerful blows on Kalia. Krishna leaped up and landed on Kalia's hood. Now, whenever Kalia Nag tried to attack Krishna with one of its head, Krishna stepped on that head and subdued it. In time, Krishna began to dance on Kalia's hoods and finally Kalia Nag surrendered to Krishna.

"Leave Yamuna and go to the ocean with your family," Krishna commanded Kalia and he did likewise.

Krishna Lifts Govardhan

Young Krishna became curious when he saw villagers making preparations for a yagya in Indra's honor. His father, Nanda explained, "Lord Indra is the god of rain and thunder. We show him our gratitude for keeping our lands green by worshipping him."

"But father, we're cowherds. Shouldn't we worship the cows that give us milk and the mountains that provide us with pastures?" reasoned Krishna.

Eventually everybody agreed with Krishna. Indra was furious and sent heavy rainfall to Vrindavan. Soon Yamuna was flooded and the flood waters threatened the villages in Vrindavan.

Krishna calmed the villagers, and then lifted the Govardhan mountain on his smallest finger and provided shelter to all the villagers and their cattle. Indra was humbled. He stopped the rain and apologized to Krishna, begging forgiveness for his arrogance.

Krishna Slays Kansa

When Kansa realized that Krishna and Balram were the sons of his sister Devaki, he sent his friend Akura to invite them to Mathura. Akura warned them about Kansa's plan.

Krishna reassured Akura, "Kansa's reign of terror is about to end."

Krishna and Balram bid farewell to their foster parents and reached Mathura. Kansa instructed his best wrestlers to fight the brothers and kill them during a match. Later, the moment Krishna and Balram entered the wrestling arena, an elephant came charging at them. As the elephant caught Krishna in its trunk, he landed punches on the elephant's head, knocking it unconscious.

Soon after, wrestlers Mushtika and Chanura challenged them for a duel.
Krishna and Balram accepted the challenge and defeated the two wrestlers.

Kansa then ordered all the wrestlers to attack Krishna and Balram in unison. The wrestlers followed the instructions but soon they were all lying unconscious in the wrestling arena. Kansa trembled with fear and tried to run away from the arena.

However, Krishna caught up with him on the dais and dragged him back to the wrestling arena. Krishna pushed Kansa onto the floor where cracks appeared. Krishna roared, "Now you will pay for your sins."

Krishna sat on Kansa and landed him blow after blow. Kansa was unable to bear the fury of Krishna's blows and died. People of Mathura rejoiced. After slaying Kansa, Krishna freed his parents, Devaki and Vasudeva from the prison. Devaki and Vasudeva rejoiced after meeting their sons.

Krishna Defeats Jarasandh

Jarasandha, the powerful ruler of Magadha, was also the father-in-law of Kansa. When he heard about Kansa's death, he swore to seek revenge against Krishna. With a large army, he attacked Mathura. Krishna and Balram led the Yadav army, fought valiantly and defeated Jarasandha. However, Jarasandha was tenacious and attacked Mathura seventeen times and was defeated each time.

In time, Krishna realized that constant battles with Jarasandha were making the life of the citizens of Mathura miserable. He therefore summoned Vishwakarma the divine architect and said, "Build me a divine city surrounded by ocean which is impregnable."

Vishwakarma built Dwarka on an island. Krishna relocated the residents of Mathura to Dwarka, where they lived a happy life and were safe from attacks.

Krishna's Peace Effort in *Mahabharata*

Duryodhana, the eldest son of Dhritarashtra hated his cousins the Pandavas, sons of his father's younger brother, Pandu. Duryodhana tricked Yudhisthira, the eldest Pandava and ruler of Indraprastha, in a game of dice. Yudhisthira lost the game and the Pandavas stayed in exile for thirteen years. After their return, Yudhisthira wanted to avoid bloodshed and sent Krishna as a peace emissary to Hastinapur.

"The Pandavas have completed their exile. It is time to return their kingdom," Krishna told King Dhritarashtra.

However, Duryodhana refused to return Indraprastha to the Pandavas. Krishna then asked for only five villages in return for peace. Duryodhana replied, "I will not give even an inch of my land to the Pandavas."

Krishna lost his patience and said, "If you don't want peace, prepare for war."

Krishna Guides and Protects Arjuna

In the Mahabharata war, Krishna was Arjuna's charioteer. When Arjuna saw Bhishma, and his teachers—Kripacharya and Drona—he cried, "How can I fight my relatives and teachers for the sake of a kingdom?"

Krishna understood Arjuna's dilemma and replied, "Dear Arjuna! There is nothing more important than following the path of righteousness. It is the warrior's duty to fight for a just cause."

He further taught Arjuna about the truths of life which now form the *Bhagwat Gita*, and revealed to Arjuna his divine cosmic form.

Arjuna's perspective changed completely. He was now ready to fight for dharma.

After the death of his son Abhimanyu, Arjuna swore to kill Jaydratha before sunset the next day. Krishna created an eclipse before sunset to lure Jaydratha out of his safety cordon. Arjuna was thus able to fulfill his vow.

To protect Arjuna, Krishna ensured that Karna used his deadliest weapon Shakti to slay Ghatotkacha, Bheema's asura son. Krishna also helped Arjuna kill Karna. After the war, Krishna asked Arjuna to step out of the chariot first. When Krishna stepped out, at once the chariot caught fire. Arjuna was perplexed. Krishna told Arjuna, "Your chariot was long destroyed by Karna. You were safe only because I was your charioteer and Hanuman resided in your flag."

Krishna and Sudama

Krishna and Sudama were childhood friends who went to the Sandipani hermitage to pursue their studies. After completing their studies, they lost touch. While Krishna became the ruler of Dwarka, Sudama married a simple girl and lived in a village. He had two children. Due to misfortunes befalling him, Sudama remained a poor man. One day, Sudama's wife reminded him of his friendship with Krishna and said, "My dear, our children will suffer and die of hunger unless you visit Krishna and ask for his help."

Sudama was embarrassed and did not want to take any favors from his friend. However, his wife convinced him that he should visit Krishna. Finally Sudama said, "Prepare some puffed rice for Krishna."

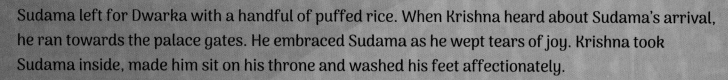

Sudama left for Dwarka with a handful of puffed rice. When Krishna heard about Sudama's arrival, he ran towards the palace gates. He embraced Sudama as he wept tears of joy. Krishna took Sudama inside, made him sit on his throne and washed his feet affectionately.

When Krishna spotted the bundle of beaten rice tied to Sudama's waist, he snatched it and quickly ate it. He then said, "My friend, I've never eaten anything so delicious in my life."

A few days later, Sudama returned home without asking Krishna for help. However when he reached home, he saw a palace where his hut stood. His wife, who welcomed him, was wearing expensive clothes. Krishna had helped his friend even though he had not asked for anything. Sudama was filled with gratitude by Krishna's love and generosity.

Krishna and Jambwanta

King Satrajit owned a very rare jewel that produced gold every day. One day, Satrajit's jewel went missing and he accused his friend, Krishna for stealing it. So, Krishna decided to prove his innocence. He learnt that Satrajit's brother had gone to the forest on a hunting expedition wearing the jewel and was killed by a lion.

The trail led Krishna to a cave where he was attacked by mighty bear Jambwanta who had fought alongside Lord Rama. An intense fight broke out between them that lasted for twenty-eight days. Jambwanta had once requested Lord Rama to duel with him. However, Lord Rama had asked him to wait until his next incarnation.

Jambwanta soon realized that his opponent was the incarnation of Lord Rama. So, he gave up the duel. He also returned the jewel which was in his possession. Krishna then granted Moksha to Jambwanta and returned the jewel to King Satrajit.

Bhishma's Vow

King Shantanu, the ruler of Hastinapur, had a son named Devavrata. One day, Devavrata noticed that his father was sad. On inquiry, he learnt that his father was in love with a woman named Satyavati.

Devavrata approached Satyavati's father and requested, "My father loves your daughter and wants to marry her. Please give your blessings to their union."

Satyavati's father replied, "The king was unwilling to assure me that Satyavati's son would become the future king of Hastinapur."

When Devavrata promised to give up his claim to the Hastinapur throne, the shrewd man replied, "What about your sons? Will they not claim the throne?"

"I take a vow of celibacy. I will never marry," said Devavrata.

After that day, Devavrata was known as Bhisma due to his terrible vow.

Drona Retrieves a Ball

Time passed. One day, the young princes of Hastinapur, were playing when their ball fell into a dry well. The princes were sad at losing the ball. Suddenly, a sage comes and says, "Why don't you fetch the ball from the well?"

The princes were confused so the sage threw his ring inside the well which fell on the ball. Next, he plucked few grass blades from the ground and chanted mantras over them. One by one, he threw the grass blades inside the well. The first grass blade pierced the ball, the second blade pierced the first. Soon a chain of grass blades emerged from the well. The sage pulled at it, until he held the ball and his ring. The astonished princes at once went and narrated the incident to their grand sire Bhishma.

Bhishma, understood that the sage was Dronacharya, and without delay appointed him as the tutor of the young princes.

Eklavya's Guru Dakshina

Eklavya, the prince of a hunter tribe, approached Dronacharya one day and requested to be his disciple. Dronacharya refused him.

Eklavya left but did not lose hope. He made a statue of Dronacharya and started practicing before it. One day, a dog started barking as he practiced. Irritated, Eklavya shot arrows that filled the dog's mouth without hurting it.

When Dronacharya and his students saw the dog, they were amazed. Soon, they found Eklavya. Curious, Dronacharya inquired about his teacher. Smiling, Eklavya touched his feet.

"He might be better than Arjuna," Dronacharya thought troubled. He then did the unthinkable, "Eklavya, as your teacher, I am also entitled to guru dakshina. I need your right thumb."

Without flinching, Eklavya cut his right thumb. Moved, Dronacharya blessed Eklavya, "You will be remembered as the greatest disciple of all time."

Duryodhana Falls In a Pool

King Dhrithrashtra split his kingdom and gave Yudhisthira, the eldest Pandava, the region of Indraprastha to rule. Demon Maya built a palace of illusions for the Pandavas. Duryodhana and some Kauravas reached Indraprastha to attend the coronation of Yudhisthira.

Duryodhana found it difficult to navigate through the palace. He bumped into a wall thinking it was a door. He mistook a crystal floor for a pool of water. In another room, he stepped forward admiring the intricate floor work when suddenly he found himself in a pool. Pandavas and Draupadi who stood nearby couldn't contain their laughter.

A humiliated Duryodhan decided to take revenge for the insult. Later he conspired with his uncle Shakuni.

Yudhisthira and Yaksha

During their exile, the Pandavas were traveling through a forest. Yudhisthira felt thirsty. Nakula went in search of water. He found a pond, and before taking some water for Yudhisthira, decided to quench his thirst first. Just as he dipped his hands in water, a voice warned him, "Answer my questions before drinking this water, else you'll die!"

Nakula ignored the warning and drank the water. He collapsed on the ground the next moment. When Nakula did not return, Yudhishtira sent Sahadeva to find their brother. Sahadeva too reached the spot and met the same fate. Bhima and Arjuna too collapsed likewise. At last, Yudhisthira himself reached the pond. He was shocked to see his brothers dead. He asked, "Who is responsible for my brothers' death? Show yourself!"

Suddenly, a Yaksha appeared before Yudhisthira and said, "This pond belongs to me. I had warned your brothers to not drink the water without answering my questions. But they were too impatient and died."

Yudhisthira agreed to answer the Yaksha's questions. "What is more important than earth?" the Yaksha asked. Yudhisthira replied, "One's mother!"

Yaksha then went on to ask Yudhisthira a lot many questions, each more difficult than the other, but Yudhisthira answered all of them correctly.

Finally, Yaksha said, "I am happy with your answers Yudhisthira. " As reward the yaksha revived all the Pandavas.

Akshay Patra

When Pandavas were living in exile, the sun god gave Yudhisthira a mystical vessel called Akshay Patra and said, "It will provide an unlimited amount of food once daily until Draupadi has eaten her fill."

One day, Sage Durvasa and his disciples were visiting Duryodhana at Hastinapur. Duryodhana was aware of Durvasa's short temper and quickness to inflict a curse. Hence, he cunningly suggested, "Oh great sage! It is unfair that my cousins are deprived of your blessings. Please visit them in the forest."

Durvasa took Duryodhana's fake concern seriously and started for the forest where he and his disciples were welcomed with the utmost respect by the Pandavas.

Durvasa blessed the Pandavas and said, "We feel extremely hungry. Please prepare a meal for us while we take a bath in the river."

Draupadi was troubled. She had eaten. The Akshay Patra would give no more food for the day. She prayed to Lord Krishna for help.

To her relief and dismay, Krishna soon entered their hut but he too was famished. He grabbed the Akshay Patra, insisting that there was still food in it. To Draupadi's surprise, Krishna picked a few grains of rice from the pot and ate them with relish. "My hunger is satisfied. Thank you for this nice meal!" he said.

Krishna, who was Narayana, was satiated and so were Sage Durvasa and his disciples. They were no longer hungry and instead returned to their ashram.

Danveer Karna

Karna was renowned for his generosity. After his morning prayers, he donated to the needy. One night, the sun god came in his dream and said, "Dear son, tomorrow Lord Indra will come and ask you for your golden armor and earrings which offer you protection against all weapons. Do not fall in his trap."

However, Karna refused to return anyone empty-handed. The next day, Lord Indra came to Karna, disguised as a sage. As Karna had expected, he asked for his armor and earrings. Karna did not hesitate to cut off his armor and earrings.

Karna's actions humbled Indra. He said, "I bow to your generosity, Karna! I am giving you the Shakti weapon but you will be able to use it only once."

Karna was Kunti's eldest son but only a handful knew this secret. Before the Mahabharata war, Krishna asked Kunti, his aunt and mother of the Pandavas, to convince Karna to join the Pandavas, his younger brothers. Kunti approached Karna after his morning prayers. She told him the secret of his birth. Karna listened to her patiently but said, "I am Radheya, the son of Radha, who had raised me lovingly after you had abandoned me."

Kunti pleaded with Karna, "I can't see my sons killing each other."

Karna smiled sadly and said, "I will spare the life of all your sons except Arjuna. During the war, one of us will die. After the war, you will still have five sons! I can't betray my friend Duryodhana."

Kunti returned to the palace guilt-ridden, dreading the future.

Karna Kills Ghatotkacha

During the Mahabharata war, Bhima summoned his mighty son Ghatotkacha, born of demoness Hidamba, to fight on their side. Ghatotkacha was incredibly powerful. He began to destroy large formations of the Kaurava army with his power. Duryodhana realized that if this continued, they might lose the battle by dawn.

So, he asked Karna to defeat Ghatotkacha. After a fearful duel, Karna realized that the only way to defeat Ghatotkacha was by using Indira's Shakti on him. He was hesitant to use it as he wanted to use it against Arjuna.

However, unable to stop Ghatotkacha. Karna used the Shakti weapon on him.

Abhimanyu

Abhimanyu was the mighty son of Arjuna and Subhadra. On the thirteenth day of battle, Arjuna was lured away elsewhere. Dronacharya knew that only Arjuna could break the Chakravyuh formation and so the Kauravas formed the dreaded Chakravyuh in his absence.

Abhimanyu approached his uncles and said, "When I was in my mother's womb, I heard my father explaining the strategy to break the different layers of a Chakravyuh. However mother fell asleep. I do not know how to come out of the formation."

Pandavas assured Abhimanyu that once they enter the Chakravyuh, they will help him exit. Brave Abhimanyu entered the Chakravyuh but Jayadratha prevented the Pandavas from entering the Chakravyuh due to a boon given to him by Lord Shiva.

Abhimanyu fought valiantly and defeated mighty warriors in the Kaurava army. He succeeded in breaking through the six tiers of the Chakravyuh. Soon, Karna engaged Abhimanyu in a fierce duel. Next, all the other Kaurava warriors including Dronacharya, Dushasana, Ashwatthama, Karna, Shakuni, Duryodhana and Kripacharya, started attacking Abhimanyu simultaneously, disregarding the rules of combat.

Abhimanyu fought valiantly until all his weapons were destroyed. In the end, Abhimanyu pulled out the wheel of his chariot and fought the Kauravas until he was ruthlessly killed.

Bhima Kills Duryodhana

As the battle neared its end, Bhima had killed all the Kauravas except Duryodhana. Duryodhana's mother Gandhari wished to protect her only remaining son.

She summoned Duryodhana and said, "Dear son, take a bath and appear in front of me without any clothes."

Duryodhana took a bath and was going to meet his mother naked when Krishna mocked him. Duryodhana was embarrassed and wrapped a banana leaf around his waist before returning to his mother.

When Gandhari finally removed her blindfold, which she had worn since her marriage, a light came out of her eyes and entered Duryodhana's body. When she saw Duryodhana, she cried, "What have you done? Due to my spiritual powers, my gaze ensured that your whole body became as strong as metal. Now, your thighs will remain vulnerable since you hid them."

On the last day of the battle, Duryodhana went inside a lake to calm his mind and body. When the Pandavas finally found him, Bhima challenged him to a duel. Soon they were locked in a fierce mace-fight. In time, Krishna sensed that Bhima was getting tired and won't succeed in defeating Duryodhana. He signalled Bhima to hit Duryodhana on his thighs. Bhima did likewise, even though it was against the rules of mace-fight.

Duryodhana was severely injured and Bhima used this opportunity to kill him by breaking his thighs. With Duryodhana's death, the Pandavas had also won the war.

Vishwamitra's Ashram

One day great Sage Vishwamitra arrived at King Dasharatha's court who was king of Ayodhaya. When Dasharatha asked the sage the purpose of his visit, Vishwamitra replied, "Asuras are defiling the altar of my yagyas. I want you to send your son Rama to protect my ashram."

Despite his hesitation, Dasharatha sent his sons Rama and Lakshmana with Sage Vishwamitra to his ashram. After leaving Ayodhaya, Vishwamitra, Rama and Lakshmana crossed the confluence of Saryu river with the Ganges and entered a dense forest. A huge demoness Tadka saw them and hurled huge boulders in their direction. Rama, with lightning speed, shot arrows and destroyed the boulders. Sensing Rama's hesitation to kill a woman, Vishwamitra said, "Rama, she is a demoness. You must kill her now."

Rama then released a divine weapon that killed Tadka. She fell down on the ground with a thud, dead.

Soon it was dusk. Rama, Lakshmana and Vishwamitra decided to rest before they continued their journey in the morning. Pleased with Rama's valor, Vishwamitra shared his knowledge of divine weapons with Rama and Lakshmana. The next day they reached Vishwamitra's ashram. In time, Vishwamitra and his disciples started the yagya as Rama and Lakshmana kept a tight vigil. The asuras charged towards the ashram but were repulsed by the arrows of Rama and Lakshmana. Rama fired a powerful dart at Maricha, a powerful asura, who fell into the ocean.

It was only when the princes killed Subahu, a powerful asura, that the other asuras fled deep into the forest never to return. Vishwamitra completed the yagya. He was pleased with the two princes and blessed them.

Ahilya's Curse

The next day Vishwamitra told Rama, "Janaka, the king of Mithila is conducting a swayamvar for his daughter Sita. Let us join in the festivities."

Soon, Vishwamitra, Rama and Lakshmana went towards Mithila. While they were going through the forest, they saw a dilapidated hut and a ruined garden before it. Rama pointed towards a statue of a woman sitting in front of the hut and asked Vishwamitra, "Reverend sage, whose statue is that? Who lived here?"

Vishwamitra said, "This hut belonged to Sage Gautam and his wife Ahilya. One day Gautam cursed his wife in anger and turned her into a statue. According to Gautam's prophecy, she can get rid of the curse when you touch her."

Rama touched the statue with respect and brought Ahilya back to life. Ahilya thanked Rama. Soon Sage Gautam arrived and was reunited with his wife.

King Janaka had invited several brave kings and princes to his daughter's swayamvar. A swayamvar was an event where a princess chose her husband from a gathering of kings and princes. Everyone was assembled in the royal court. A large bow was kept in the center of the court.

King Janaka addressed everyone saying, "I welcome all the brave warriors to the swayamvar of my daughter, Sita. The bow that you see was given to my ancestors by Lord Shiva. Sita will marry the person who can lift and string this bow."

One by one, the assembled kings and princes tried to lift the bow but it was too heavy for them. In the end, Sage Vishwamitra asked Rama to lift the bow. Rama lifted the bow with ease. But when Rama tried to string it, the bow broke into two making a thunderous sound. Rama had won and Sita was married to him.

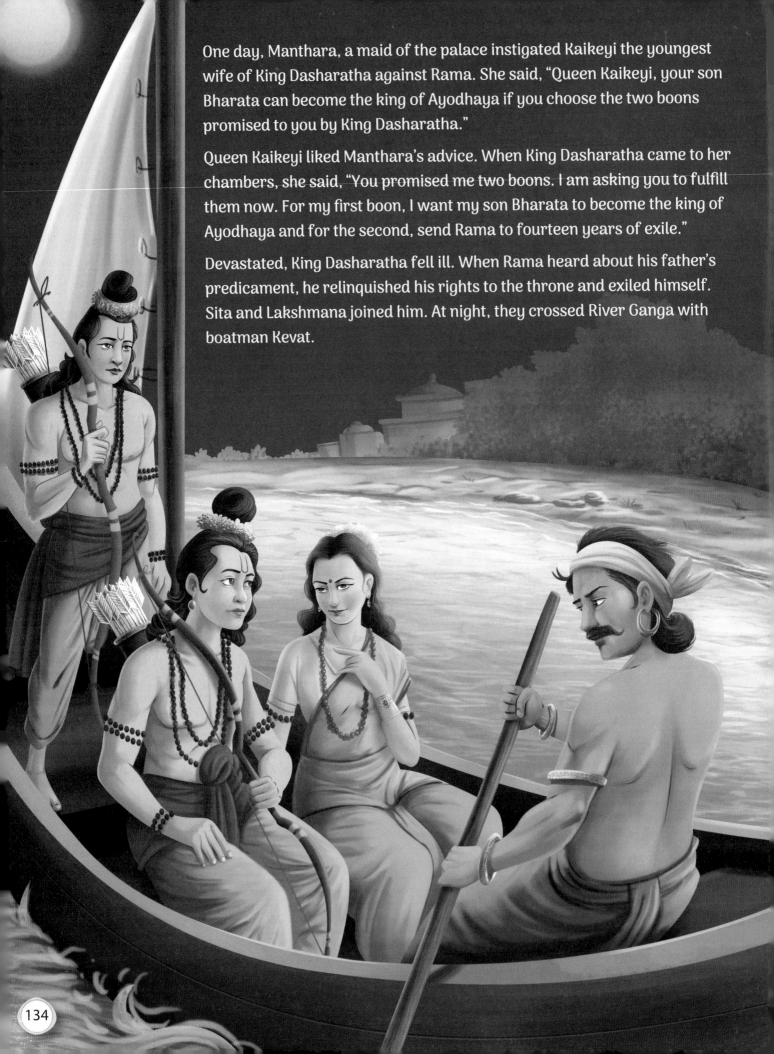

One day, Manthara, a maid of the palace instigated Kaikeyi the youngest wife of King Dasharatha against Rama. She said, "Queen Kaikeyi, your son Bharata can become the king of Ayodhaya if you choose the two boons promised to you by King Dasharatha."

Queen Kaikeyi liked Manthara's advice. When King Dasharatha came to her chambers, she said, "You promised me two boons. I am asking you to fulfill them now. For my first boon, I want my son Bharata to become the king of Ayodhaya and for the second, send Rama to fourteen years of exile."

Devastated, King Dasharatha fell ill. When Rama heard about his father's predicament, he relinquished his rights to the throne and exiled himself. Sita and Lakshmana joined him. At night, they crossed River Ganga with boatman Kevat.

Rama, Lakshmana and Sita settled down in the beautiful Chitrakoot forest. One day Bharata approached the hut leading a small contingent of soldiers. Rama welcomed Bharata and asked, "Why do you look so sad? What is the matter?"

Bharata informed Rama that their father King Dasharatha had passed away. Rama was filled with grief and it was a while before he could regain his composure. "I don't want to be king. Please return to Ayodhaya with me," Bharata pleaded.

Filled with grief, Rama resolutely said, "We belong to the Raghu clan. We can sacrifice our lives to keep our promises but never go back on them."

Bharata then said, "If that is what you wish brother, then give me your footwear. I will place it on the throne and rule Ayodhaya on your behalf while living as an ascetic."

Rama agreed. Soon, Bharata returned to Ayodhaya carrying Rama's footwear on his head.

A few years later, Rama, Lakshmana and Sita started living in Panchavati near River Godavari. One day demoness Supranakha saw Rama and was attracted to him. She disguised her appearance, approached Rama and said, "My name is Supranakha. The moment I saw you, I decided to marry you."

Rama smiled and said, "I am married and living with my wife Sita. You can marry my brother Lakshmana who is living alone at the moment."

When Supranakha proposed to marry Lakshmana, he too refused her. Supranakha felt insulted. She tried to attack Sita but Lakshmana intervened quickly to protect her. He took out his dagger and cut off Supranakha's nose. Supranakha howled in pain and ran away.

Supranakha went to her brother Ravana in Lanka and said in an agonised voice, "Look at me. I am the sister of the king of Lanka but I was humiliated by a human Rama and his brother Lakshmana. You must avenge my humiliation." She narrated all that had happened to Ravana and added that Rama's wife Sita was a divine beauty and was fit to be his new queen.

Ravana was furious and decided to abduct Sita. He approached the asura Maricha, who had magical powers, and sought his help to abduct Sita. Though reluctant, Maricha agreed to help Ravana. He transformed into a golden deer and came close to Rama's cottage.

Sita saw the deer and said to Rama, "I have never seen such a beautiful deer. Please catch the deer and bring it to me."

Lakshmana was suspicious and said, "It does not look like an ordinary deer. I think it is an asura disguised as one."

Rama was, however, unable to refuse Sita's request. Before he left, he commanded Lakshmana, "Guard Sita. Do not leave her alone till I return."

Lakshmana stood guard outside their hut. Meanwhile, the deer enticed Rama deep into the forest. Finally Rama shot an arrow which pierced the deer's heart. In that moment, Maricha regained his true form. He mimicked Rama's voice and cried, "Lakshmana, save me. Help!"

Sita heard the cry. Worried for Rama's safety, she pleaded with Lakshmana to go and protect his brother. Lakshmana left reluctantly.

When Lakshmana left, Ravana seized the opportunity and abducted Sita.

Rama was surprised to see his brother. It was then that they realized that they had been tricked and rushed back to the cottage. Rama was distraught when he couldn't find Sita. Lakshmana was grief-stricken.

The two brothers wandered in the forest in search of Sita. Eventually they found the old mighty vulture Jatayu who was mortally wounded lying on the ground. Before his breathe left him, Jatayu apologised to Rama at his inability to save Sita from the clutches of evil Ravana.

In time, they reached Shabri's cottage. She had been awaiting their arrival. She offered Rama berries, which she first tasted herself to give him the sweetest.

Shabri tells them to reach Rishyamukha mountain where they will get help in Sugreeva. Sugreeva was a powerful monkey warrior and son of Surya, the sun god. Sugreeva had made the mountain his abode after he had been banished by his brother Vali, the ruler of Kishkinda. Sugreeva was aided by Hanuman, son of the wind god Vayu. Hanuman was elated when he finally met Lord Rama. He introduced Rama and Lakshmana to Sugreeva.

Sugreeva and Rama formed an alliance. Rama assured Sugreeva that he would kill Vali, Sugreeva's brother. In return, Sugreeva promised Rama his assistance in finding Sita. Soon, Sugreeva challenged Vali to a duel. Vali accepted the challenge.

During the fierce duel, Lord Rama, stayed hidden, and shot an arrow at Vali. Vali died. Sugreeva was crowned the king of Kishkinda.

After becoming king, Sugreeva sent vanara teams in different directions to locate Sita. Eventually, Hanuman managed to locate Sita in Lanka, an island nation in the sea. After setting Lanka on fire, Hanuman returned and narrated his adventures to Lord Rama. With the help of Sugreeva, Lord Rama led a huge army of vanaras towards Lanka. Finally they reached the seashore. Lord Rama worshipped Varuna, the ocean god and requested him to create a path in the water but he did not appear. Lord Rama became furious and decided to make the ocean dry.

Varuna emerged afraid and said, "There are two vanaras with you, Nala and Neer. They have a boon where any object that they will throw in the water will not sink. Use their boon to create a bridge to Lanka."

The vanara army at once set to work. They found boulders, gave them to Nala and Neer who would throw them in the water. In time, a bridge was made to reach Lanka.

A fierce battle broke out between Rama's army and the asuras. Rama, Lakshmana, Hanuman, Sugreeva killed several powerful asuras. Ravana was desperate and decided to wake up his younger brother Kumbhakaran immediately. Kumbhakaran woke up after a lot of toil. Kumbhakaran met Ravana and asked, "Why did you wake me up?" According to a boon Kumbhakaran slept for six months.

Ravana explained the situation to Kumbhakaran and ordered him to kill Rama. Kumbhakaran reassured his elder brother and went to the battlefield. He wreaked havoc on Rama's army and even captured Sugreeva. Finally Rama challenged Kumbhakaran to a duel. After a fierce battle Rama invoked divine weapons and brought an end to Kumbhakaran.

The asuras were demoralised after Kumbhakaran's death and fled the battlefield.

Hanuman Proves His Devotion

Ravana was shattered when he heard about Kumbhakaran's death. Ravana's son Indrajeet promised his father, "I will kill both the brothers and crush their army."

Indrajeet and Lakshmana fought viciously. After a tough fought battle that had many illusions created by Indrajeet, Lakshmana eventually killed him. It was then that Ravana came to the battlefield and attacked Rama's army. Rama did not hesitate even for a moment and engaged Ravana in a fierce battle. Despite his best efforts, Rama was unable to defeat Ravana. Rama then learnt the secret to Ravana's death from Vibhishan, Ravana's younger brother, "Aim your weapon at his naval."

Rama then fired the divine Brahmastra which pierced Ravana's naval, killing him instantly. The asura army surrendered after the death of their king.

Rama entered Lanka and was reunited with Sita. Rama thanked Vibhishan for his help in defeating Ravana. He crowned Vibhishan as the new king of Lanka.

Rama's fourteen years of exile was also coming to an end by this time. Rama then summoned Hanuman and said, "Go to my brother Bharata in Ayodhaya. Tell him that I shall be arriving soon. He had sworn to renounce his life if I didn't reach Ayodhaya when my exile ended."

Hanuman flew to Ayodhaya and conveyed Rama's message to Bharata. Bharata was elated. Rama was crowned the king of Ayodhaya. Hanuman stayed in Ayodhaya to serve Rama. Ayodhaya's prosperity reached its zenith under Rama's reign.

The Fire Pillar

After the creation of the universe, Lord Vishnu was lost in deep meditation. As time passed, a large lotus emerged from his navel. There was a golden egg inside the lotus. When the egg cracked, Lord Brahma emerged from it. He was surprised to see Lord Vishnu. Sensing Lord Brahma's presence, Lord Vishnu opened his eyes and said, "I am Vishnu, the supreme god of this universe. Who are you?"

Lord Brahma replied, "I am Brahma, the god of knowledge and creation. I am the supreme god of the universe."

The two gods argued for a long time and finally decided to duel to establish their supremacy over the other. They hurled devastating weapons at each other but no winner emerged. Suddenly, a pillar of fire appeared out of nowhere. Their weapons disappeared in it and Lord Shiva emerged out of the pillar.

The Contest

Lord Shiva commanded, "Stop or you will destroy the universe I have created. Why are you fighting?"

Both Lord Brahma and Lord Vishnu staked their claim to be acknowledged as the supreme god of the universe; after all, they were both mighty.

Lord Shiva smiled and decided to teach them a lesson in humility. He pointed to the pillar and said, "There is an easy way to resolve this quarrel. How about a contest? Whoever reaches the top or bottom of this fire pillar first shall be declared the supreme god of this universe."

Both the gods agreed. Lord Vishnu transformed into a boar and began to dig the ground in order to reach the bottom of the pillar. Lord Brahma transformed into a swan and flew up high in the sky to find the top.

Lord Vishnu continued to dig for a long time, but was unable to find the bottom of the fire pillar. So, he decided to go back and accept defeat.

Meanwhile, Lord Brahma was unable to find the top of the pillar despite his best efforts. He was ready to concede defeat when he spotted a *Ketaki* flower. Lord Brahma returned holding the flower in his hand. He showed it to Lord Shiva and said, "I found this *Ketaki* flower at the top of the fire pillar. I have won this contest." Lord Vishnu, on the other hand, spoke the truth and accepted defeat.

Lord Shiva was furious with Lord Brahma and put a curse on him, "You should not have lied! As you have spoken a lie you will not be worshipped by anyone." Pleased with Lord Vishnu's humility, he said, "You shall have the same status as me in this universe."

Daksha Humiliates Shiva

Daksha was the son of Brahma. After appeasing the divine mother, Adishakti, he was blessed with a girl, whom he named Sati. When Sati grew up, she wanted to marry Lord Shiva. She appeased him with severe penance and Lord Shiva agreed to marry her. Arrogant Daksha agreed to the marriage reluctantly and Sati married Lord Shiva.

One day, Daksha organized a yajna at Prayag. Several sages, gods and Lord Shiva were invited to it. When Daksha entered the *yajnashala*, everyone except Lord Shiva stood up to greet him. Daksha was extremely offended by this behavior. He humiliated Lord Shiva saying, "I banish you from this ritual. From now on, no one will ever make an offering to you in a yajna."

Lord Shiva was saddened to see Daksha's misbehavior and left.

Sati

Daksha wanted to humiliate Lord Shiva further. So, he organized another grand yajna. He invited everyone except Lord Shiva and Sati. When Sati found out about the yagna, she was hurt and decided to confront her father.

Lord Shiva cautioned her, "You should not go if you are not invited. I advise you to go after the ceremony is over."

Sati replied, "Why would a daughter need an invitation to visit her own parents' house? I want to attend the yajna!"

When Lord Shiva saw that Sati was determined, he summoned Nandi and a few other *Ganas* to escort Sati to her parents' home.

Daksha was not happy to see Sati at the yajna. She immediately confronted him when she saw that there was no offering made to Lord Shiva.

Daksha did not mask his hatred for Lord Shiva and said, "I did not invite you to this yajna. Why have you come? Your husband is an imposter, he has no regard for our traditions, our holy books and he keeps objectionable company. He is not fit to receive our offerings."

Unable to withstand her husband's insult Sati wept and said, "I disobeyed my husband and came here, hoping that you would listen to me. However, you have insulted him right before me. I'm ashamed to be your daughter."

Filled with endless grief, remorse and humiliation, Sati invoked a yogic fire and renounced her life.

Shiva's Retribution

Lord Shiva was worried when he saw Nandi return alone, weeping. His heart filled with grief when Nandi told him about Sati's demise. Soon, the grief gave way to rage. Lord Shiva assumed his darkest and most savage form, Veerbhadra. He led an army of his *Ganas* and attacked Daksha and others who were present at the yajna.

Sensing danger, Daksha prayed to Lord Vishnu and asked him to protect his guests from Shiva's wrath. Lord Vishnu agreed to help. As he fought Lord Shiva, he also pleaded with him to spare the innocent lives of the guests.

Lord Shiva accepted this request and stopped fighting. Lord Shiva saw Daksha hiding and decided to punish him alone.

Lord Shiva rushed towards Daksha, beheaded him with a single blow and threw his head in the holy fire. His anger only subsided when he saw Sati's corpse. Dropping his weapon, he embraced her listless body and began weeping.

After a while, the benevolent Shiva, at the request of Daksha's wife, revived Daksha. As Daksha's head was destroyed, Lord Shiva replaced the head with that of a goat. Without delay, Daksha begged for Lord Shiva's forgiveness the minute he came to life.

Lord Shiva forgave him and left. He roamed the earth like a nomad, hoping to be reunited with his beloved one day.

Shiva's Wrath

After a very long time, Sati was reincarnated as Parvati, the daughter of King Himavan and Queen Maina. One day, Lord Shiva came to King Himavan's kingdom and said, "I wish to meditate in solitude." King Himavan assured Lord Shiva that he would not be disturbed. While Shiva meditated, Parvati brought him fruits each day.

Meanwhile, the demon Tarakasur had become the king of heaven. Due to a boon from Lord Brahma, he could only be killed by Shiva's son. So, Lord Indra summoned Kamadev, the god of love, and asked him to move Lord Shiva such that he agrees to marry Parvati. Kamadev fired his *Kamaban*, a magical arrow of love, at Lord Shiva precisely when Parvati arrived. Lord Shiva felt an instant attraction for Parvati. But he also realized why that was. Furious, he reduced Kamadev to ashes.

Shiva and Parvati

Lord Shiva left the meditation site in anger and was pacified only when the gods apologized for interfering in his life. Parvati was scared after witnessing Lord Shiva's fury. She was unsure whether or not he would accept her as his wife.

One day, Sage Narad met Parvati and said, "Lord Shiva is an ascetic and can be appeased only by penance."

So, Parvati performed an austere penance and finally, Lord Shiva appeared and agreed to marry her. She asked him to meet her parents.

Lord Shiva arrived at King Himavan's palace, disguised as Natraj, an ordinary street dancer. Parvati recognized him instantly, as he enthralled the audience with his divine dance.

When the performance was over, Queen Maina offered him gold ornaments as a reward. However, Lord Shiva refused and said, "I only seek your daughter's hand as my reward."

King Himavan and Queen Maina were furious upon hearing this request from a stranger. Then, Parvati requested Lord Shiva to reveal his true form. Upon seeing Shiva, King Himavan and Queen Maina accepted his proposal immediately.

Lord Shiva and Parvati were married in a grand ceremony. After the wedding, Lord Shiva resurrected Kamadev from his ashes and forgave him.

Andhak

One day, Goddess Parvati playfully closed Lord Shiva's eyes with her hands while he was meditating on Mount Mandara. The entire universe got covered with darkness as Lord Shiva was blinded. Droplets of sweat from Parvati's hands fell on the ground and a blind boy was born there. The divine couple named him Andhak. They gave the boy to Hiranyaksha, who had been praying to them for a child.

Andhak was always ill-treated by his cousins due to his divine birth. So, he meditated and prayed to Lord Brahma. Pleased with his devotion, Lord Brahma appeared before him and offered him a boon. Andhak replied, "I want my eyesight restored, and I pray that I can only be killed if I wish to marry a woman who is like a mother to me." He thought that this would make him immortal.

Brahma granted Andhak this boon.

Andhak had become invincible due to his boon. He even invaded heaven and dethroned Indra. In no time, he had become the ruler of the three worlds.

One day, Andhak was exploring Mount Mandara with his generals. The generals spotted Lord Shiva meditating in a cave with Goddess Parvati. They did not recognize the divine couple. The generals came back to Andhak and described Parvati as the most beautiful woman in the universe, fit to become his wife. So, Andhak sent his army to fight Lord Shiva. During the battle, he tried to kidnap Goddess Parvati. However, Shiva struck him with his trident and lifted him in the air. Andhak realized his mistake and repented for his sins. Lord Shiva forgave him and turned him into a *Gana* chief.

Markandeya

Sage Mrikandu and his wife Marudwati prayed to Lord Shiva to bless them with a child. Pleased with their devotion, Lord Shiva appeared before Sage Mrikandu and said, "I bless you with an intelligent son, but he will only live for sixteen years."

Soon, Sage Mrikandu and Marudwati were blessed with a son. They named him Markandeya. In time, Sage Mrikandu told his son about his approaching death.

Shocked but resolute, Markandeya built a *Shivalinga* and began to worship Lord Shiva with great devotion. On his sixteenth birthday, he was singing a bhajan when Yamraj appeared to take him.

In response, Markandeya clung to the *Shivalinga*. At once, Lord Shiva appeared from within the *Shivalinga*, and said, "Don't touch this boy! He is my devotee."

Yamraj went away, and Markandeya lived a long and virtuous life.

Shiva and Arjun

One day, Arjun was worshipping Lord Shiva before a *Shivalinga* when suddenly, a wild boar charged at him. Arjun quickly shot an arrow, killing it instantly. He, however, was surprised to see a second arrow stuck in the boar's body.

A tribal chief approached Arjun and argued that it was his arrow that had killed the boar. The chief's wife suggested that they duel to settle the argument. Arjun fought skillfully but was unable to defeat the chief. Finally, he made a garland of flowers and placed it around the *Shivalinga* to seek Lord Shiva's blessings.

To his surprise, the same garland appeared around the tribal chief's neck. Arjuna was humbled and bowed to Lord Shiva.